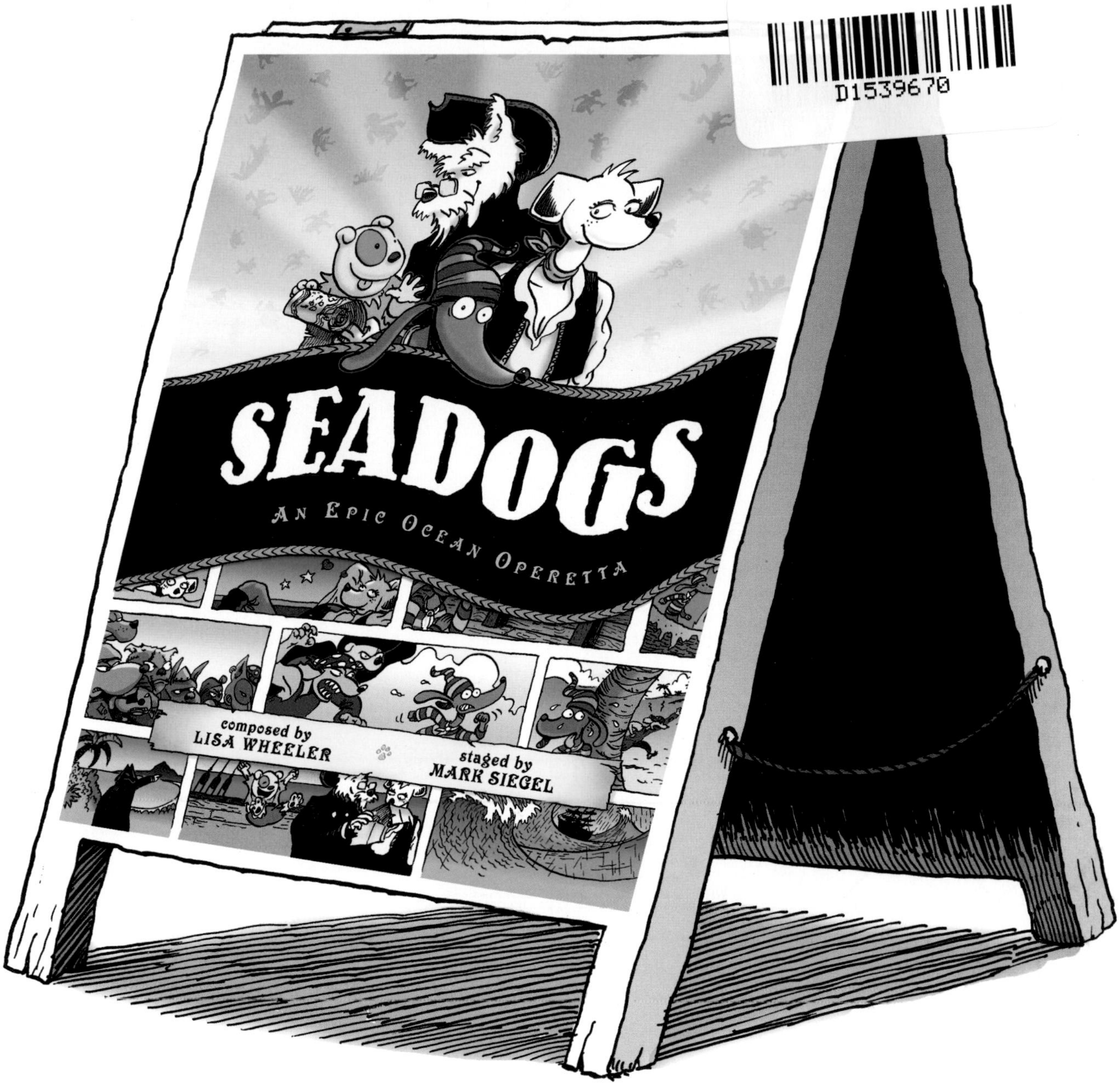
SEADOGS
An Epic Ocean Operetta
composed by
LISA WHEELER
staged by
MARK SIEGEL

For Uncle Bill, Grandpa Oggie, and Papa Bob—seadogs, three—
and Shane, my pup
—L. W.

For you, Siena
—M. S.

Aladdin Paperbacks
New York London Toronto Sydney

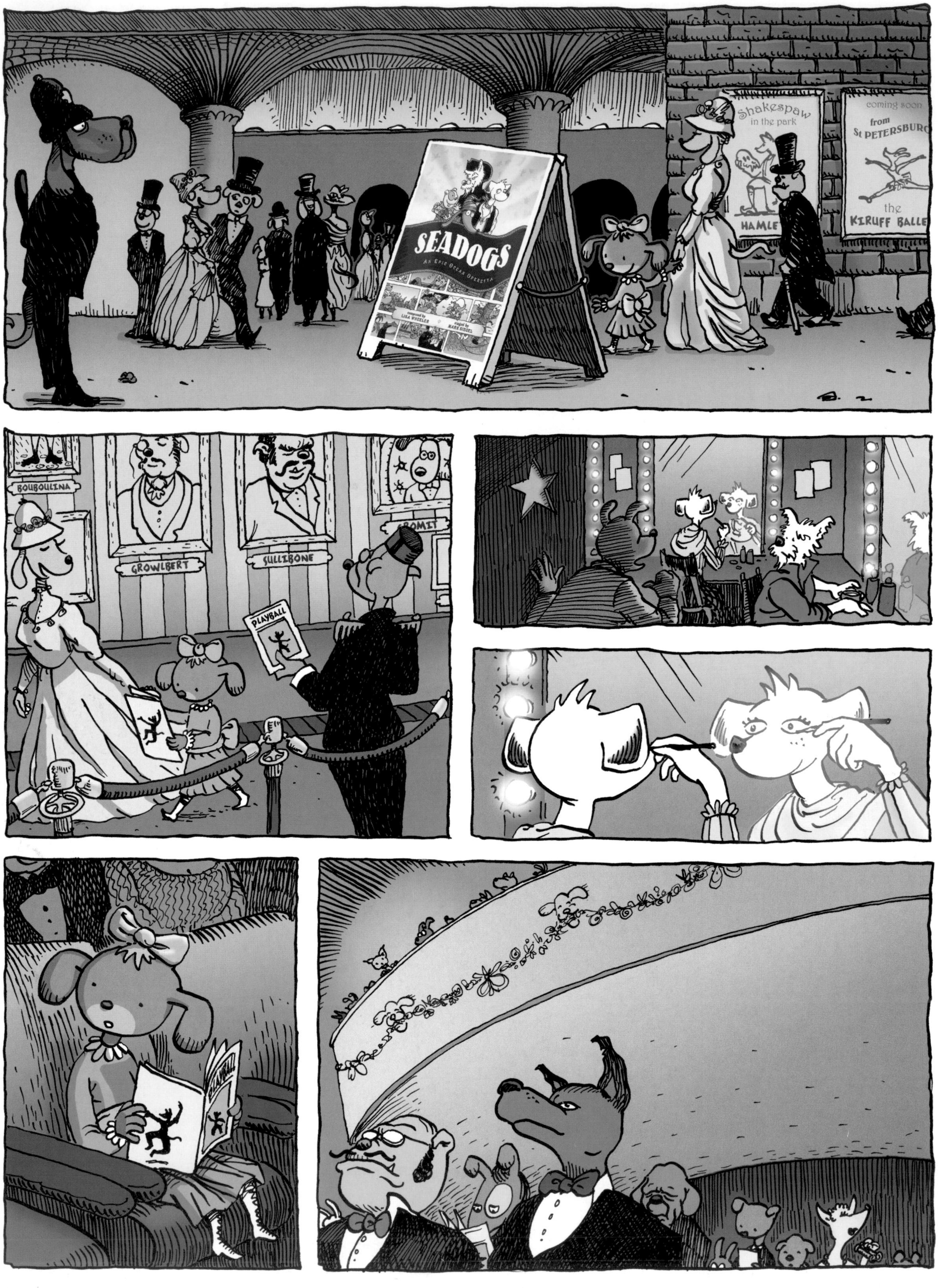
SEADOGS
Shakespaw
in the park
HAMLE
coming soon
from
St PETERSBUR
the
KIRUFF BALLE
BOUBOULINA
GROWLBERT
SULLIBONE
ROMIT
PLAYBALL
PLAYBALL

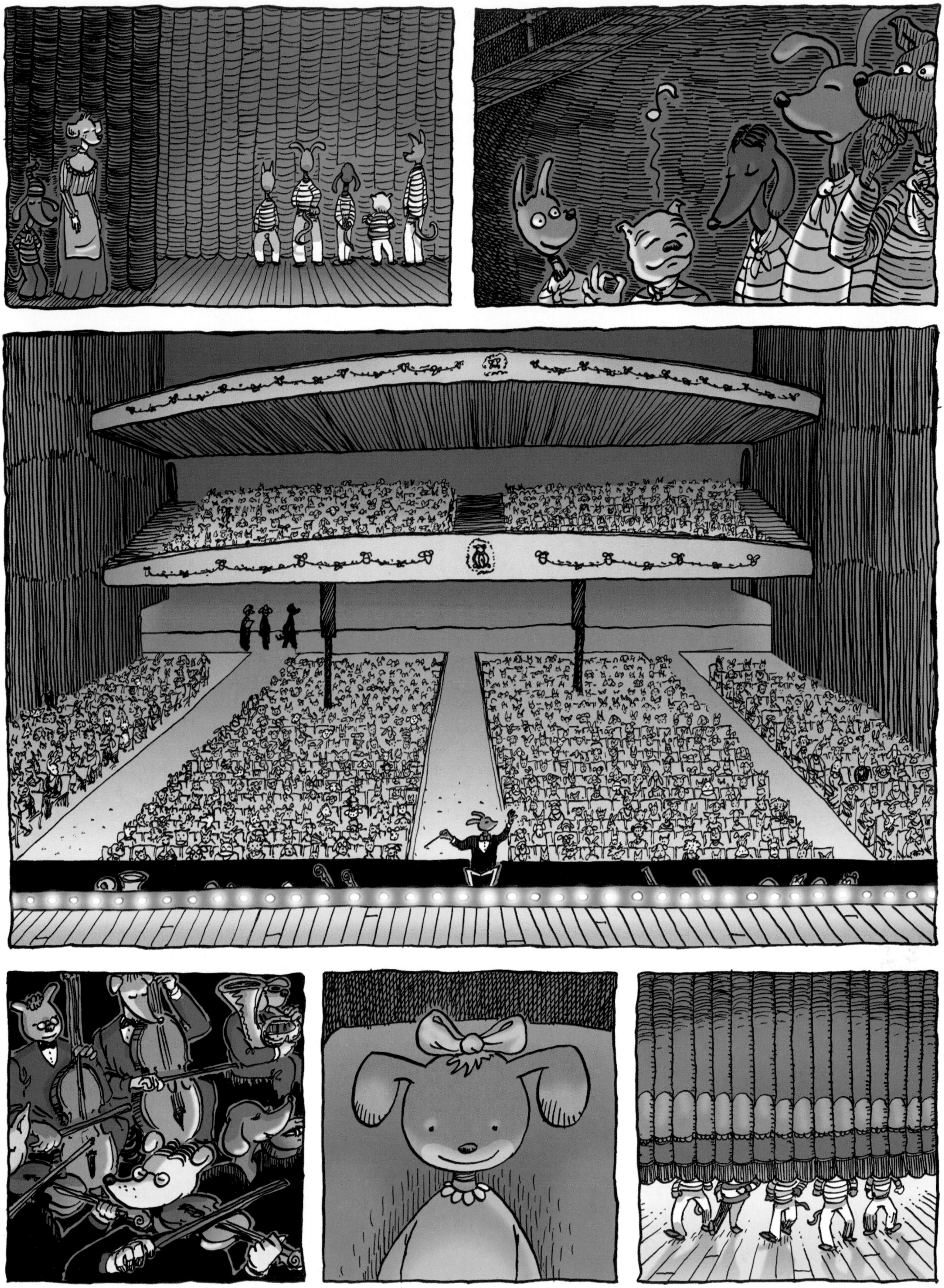

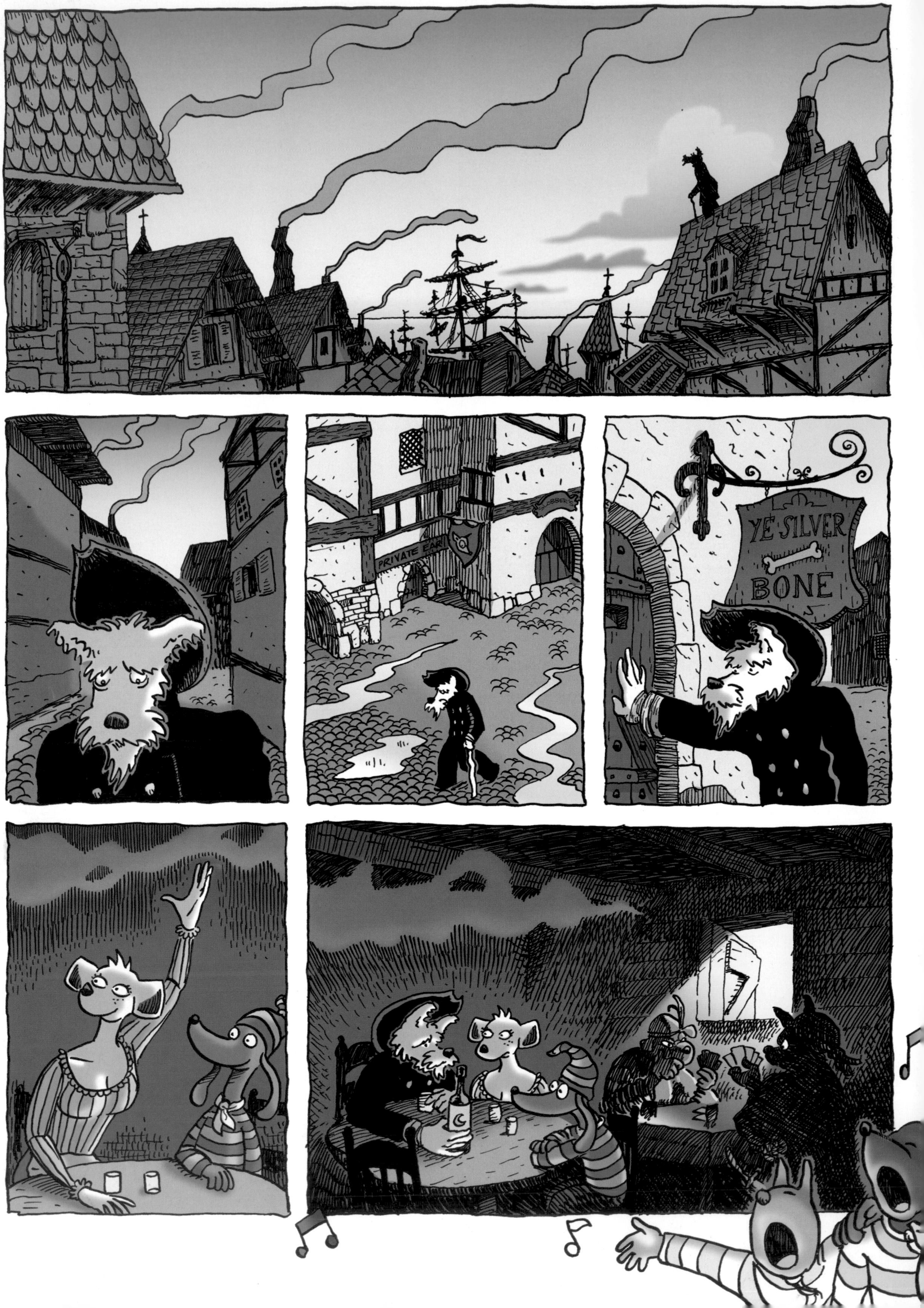
PRIVATE EAR
YE SILVER BONE

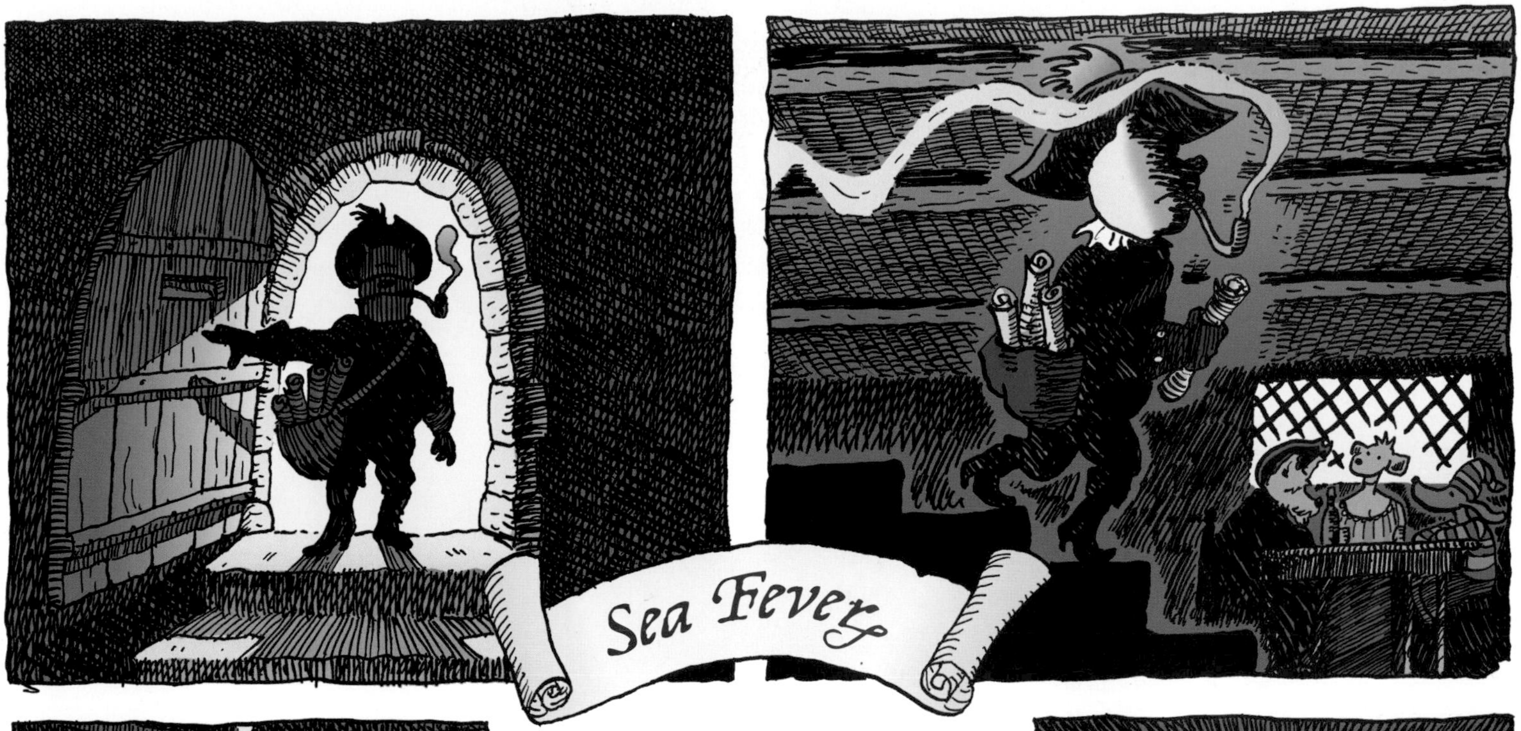
Sea Fever

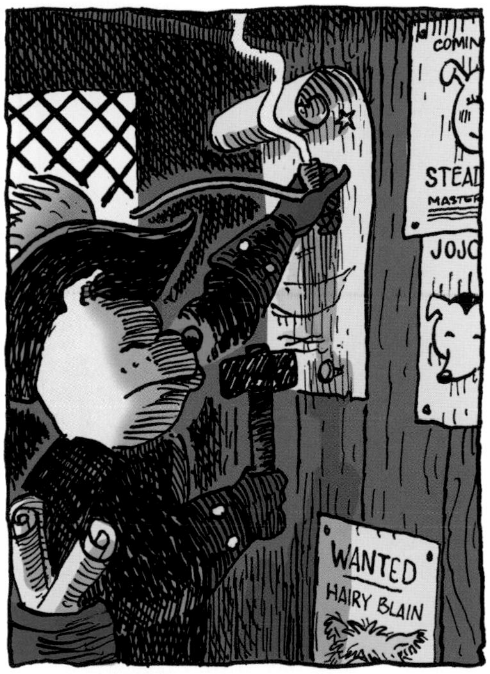
WANTED
HAIRY BLAIN

Old Seadog yowls
a lonesome cry,
a homesick howl
for surf
and sky,
a yearning
he cannot deny. . . .

And all he asks
is a tall, tall ship
and a star to steer her by.

(WITH SINCEREST RESPECT FOR
JOHN MASEFIELD, 1878–1967)

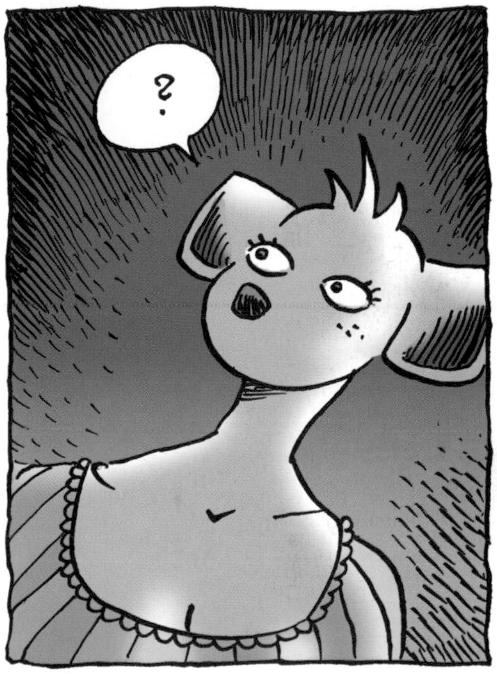
?

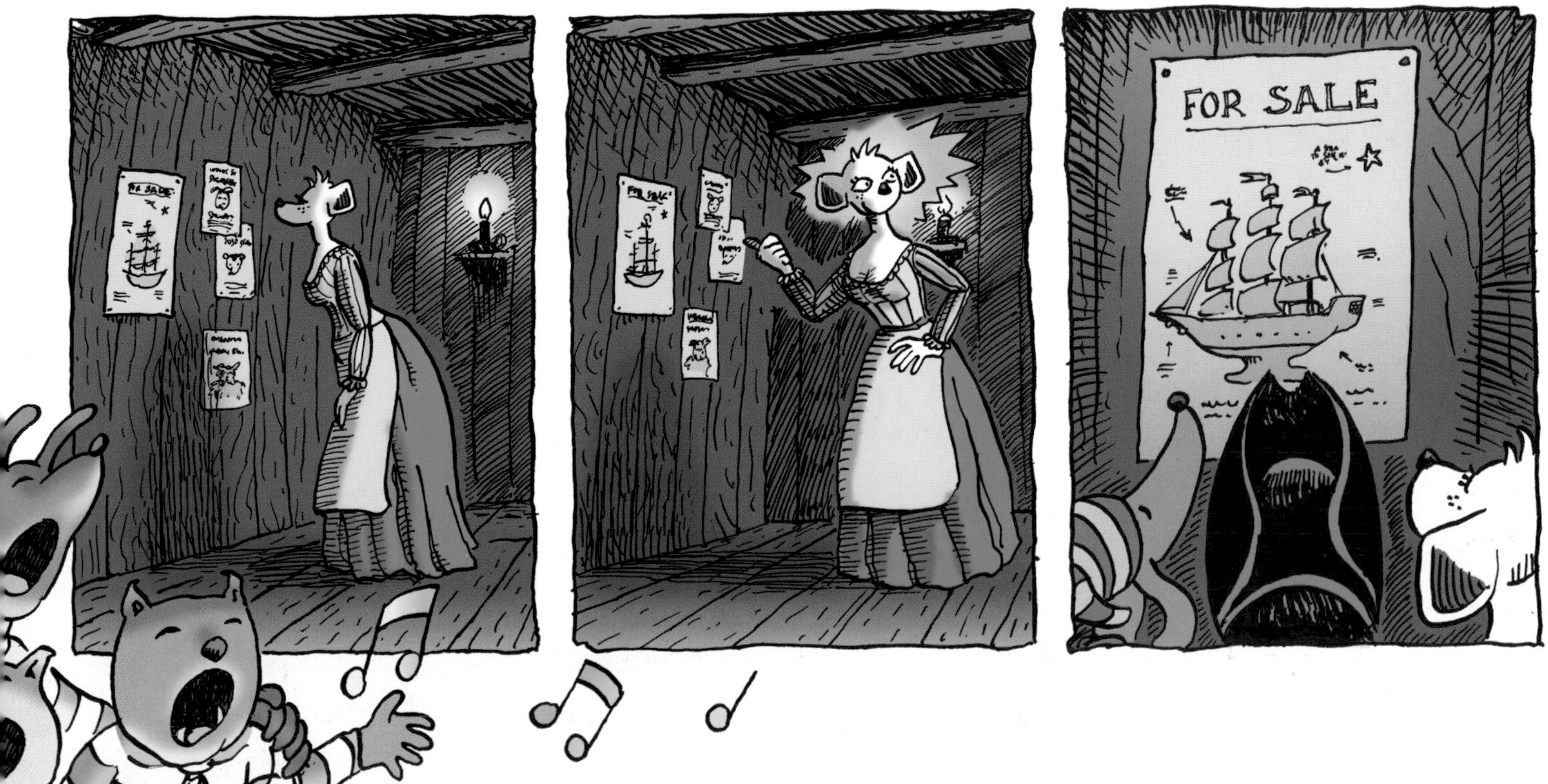
FOR SALE

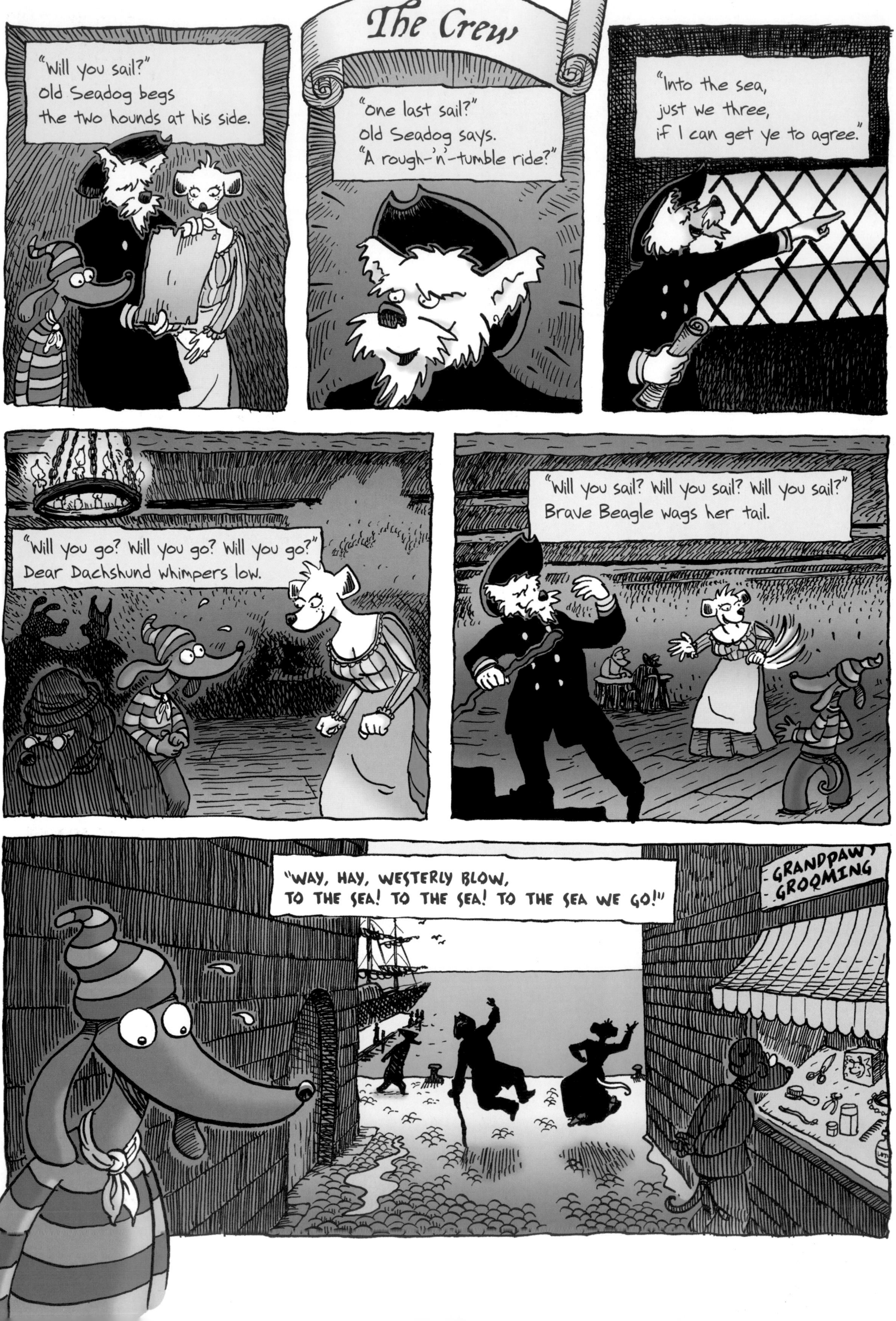
The Crew
"Will you sail?" Old Seadog begs the two hounds at his side.
"One last sail?" Old Seadog says. "A rough-'n'-tumble ride?"
"Into the sea, just we three, if I can get ye to agree."
"Will you go? Will you go? Will you go?" Dear Dachshund whimpers low.
"Will you sail? Will you sail? Will you sail?" Brave Beagle wags her tail.
"WAY, HAY, WESTERLY BLOW, TO THE SEA! TO THE SEA! TO THE SEA WE GO!"
GRANDPAWS GROOMING

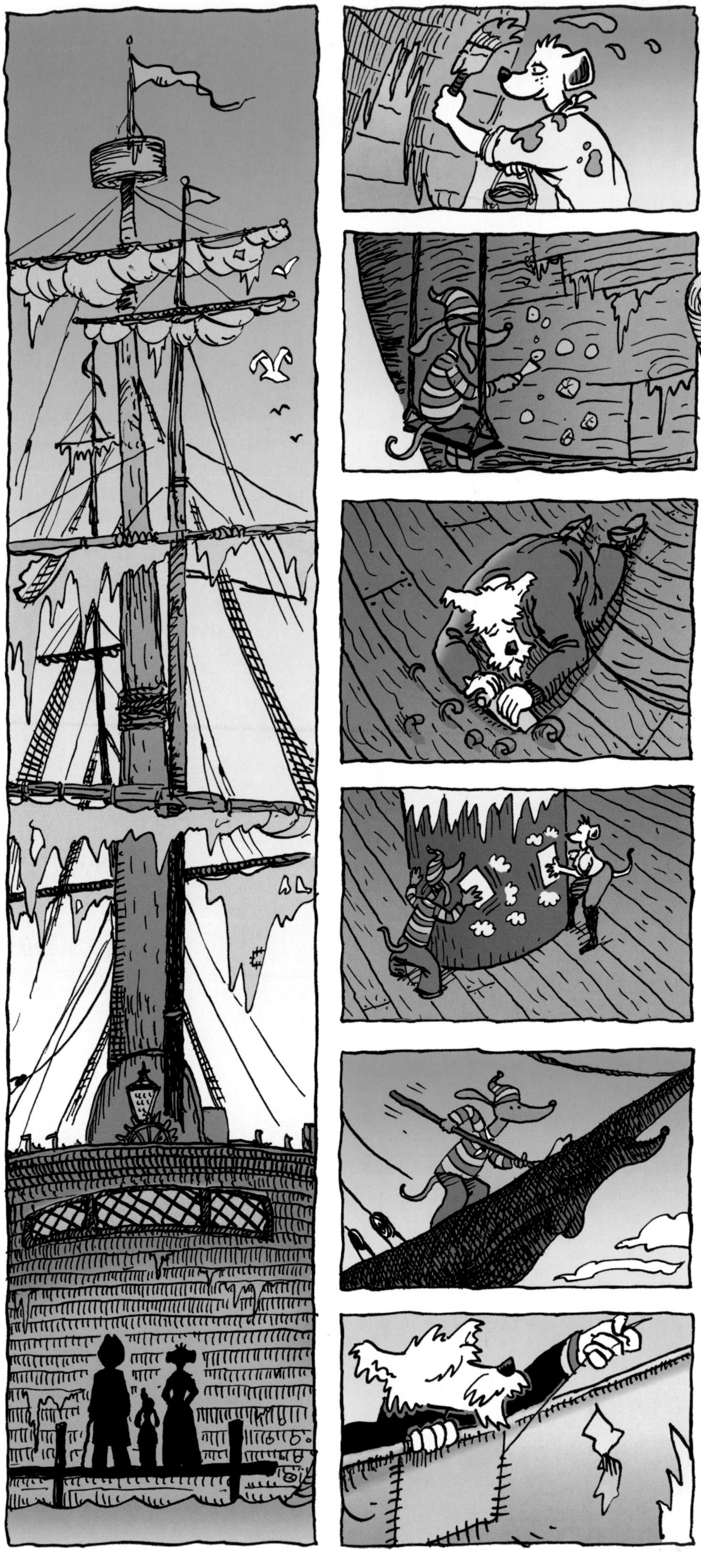

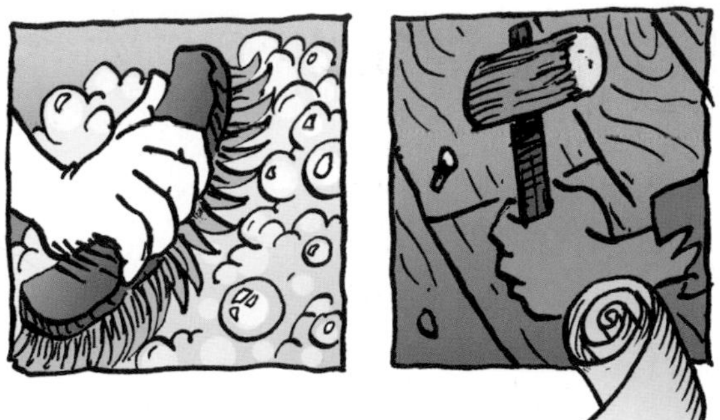

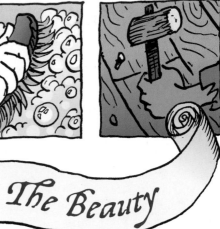

The Beauty

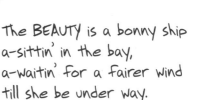

The BEAUTY is a bonny ship
a-sittin' in the bay,
a-waitin' for a fairer wind
till she be under way.

Then fare you well, ol' Corgytown,
fare you well, we sing.
We're off to find adventure where
a dog can be a King!

We tar her hull with pine and pitch.
We shine the bosun's bell.
We scrape off all the barnacles
'cause they don't suit her well.

Then fare you well, ol' Corgytown,
fare you well, we sing.
We're off to find adventure where
a dog can be a King!

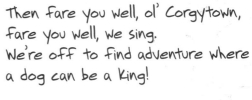

We sand and paint the mizzenmast.
We mend the flags and sheets.
We fill her mess with hearty drink
and all the choicest meats.

Then fare you well, ol' Corgytown,
fare you well, we sing.
We're off to find adventure where
a dog can be a King!

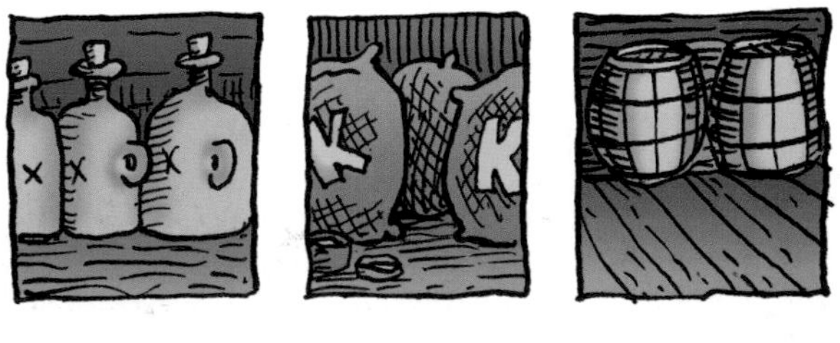

To the Sea

"Cast the lines!
Unfurl the sails!
Lift your ears!
Uncurl your tails!"

Old Seadog shouts out from the rails.

"Trim the jib!
Hoist the main!"
The crew of two
does not complain.

Old Seadog's head of this domain.

Zephyr wind
and salty air,
ruffled fur
and tousled hair.
Their destination?
Anywhere!

Old Seadog offers up a prayer.

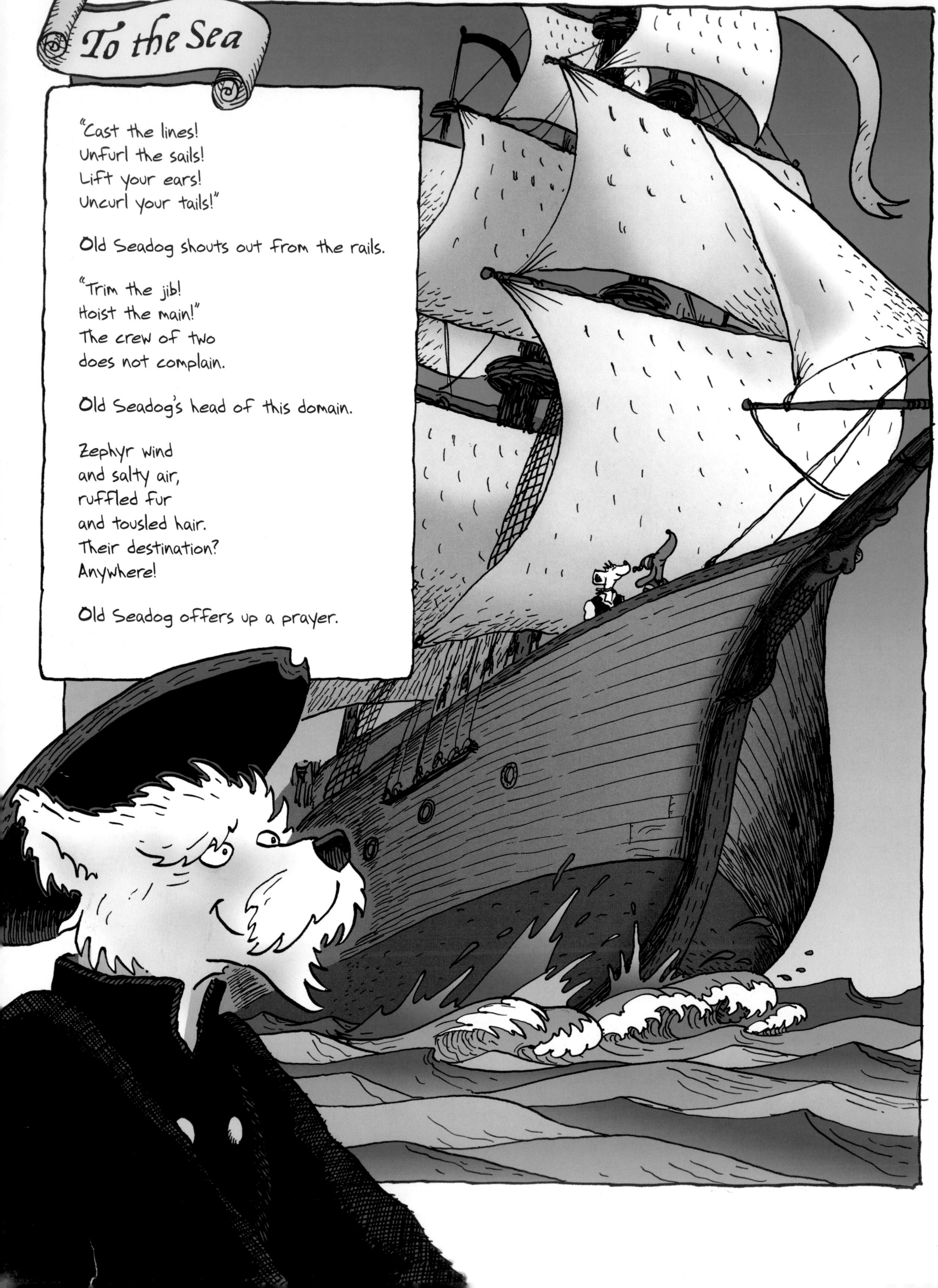

Brave Beagle Wasn't Always Brave. . . .

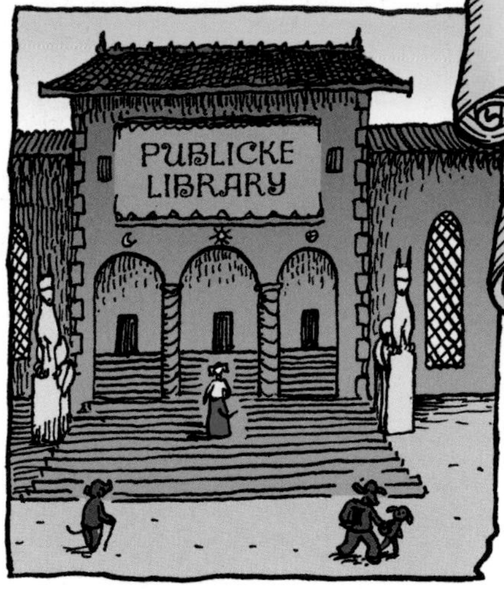
PUBLICKE LIBRARY

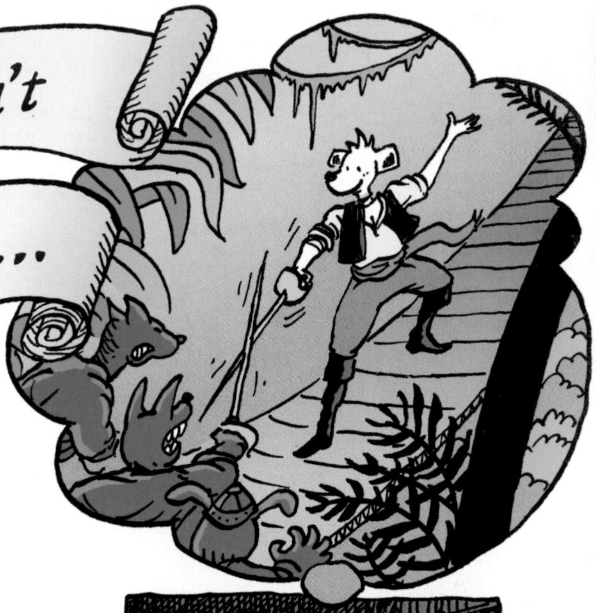

But then she joined a scurvy crew,
cut her teeth in Timbuktu,
trained and tamed the ocean blue.
'Twas lonely years and
longing, too,
that made Brave Beagle brave.

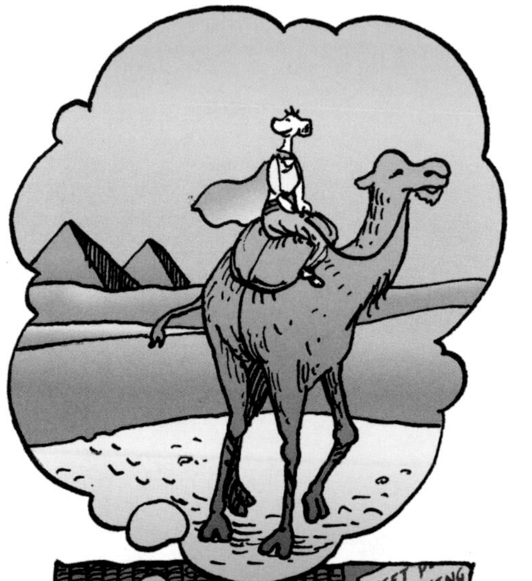

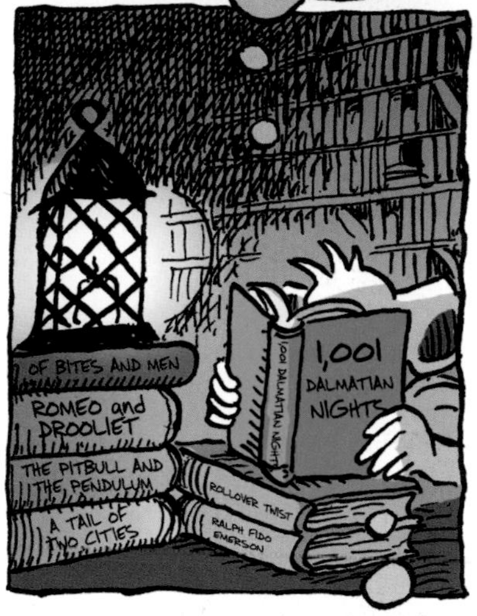
OF BITES AND MEN
ROMEO and DROOLIET
THE PITBULL AND THE PENDULUM
A TAIL OF TWO CITIES
1,001 DALMATIAN NIGHTS
ROLLOVER TWIST
RALPH FIDO EMERSON

Brave Beagle wasn't always brave. . . .

But then she sailed the seven seas,
battled mange and tackled fleas,
brought a wolf pack to its knees.
'Twas years of fearsome
deeds like these
that made Brave Beagle brave.

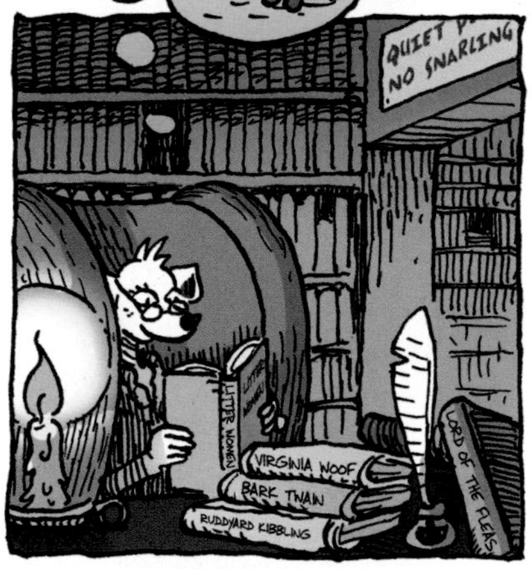
NO SNARLING
VIRGINIA NOOF
BARK TWAIN
RUDDYARD KIBBLING
LORD OF THE FLEAS

Brave Beagle wasn't always brave. . . .

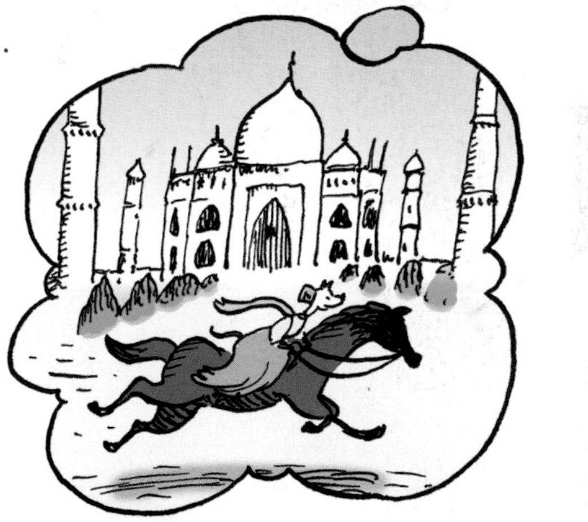

But then she met a dachshund, dear,
a sweet, reluctant volunteer,
who charmed the erstwhile buccaneer.
'Twas love that taught
her heart to fear
and made Brave Beagle brave.

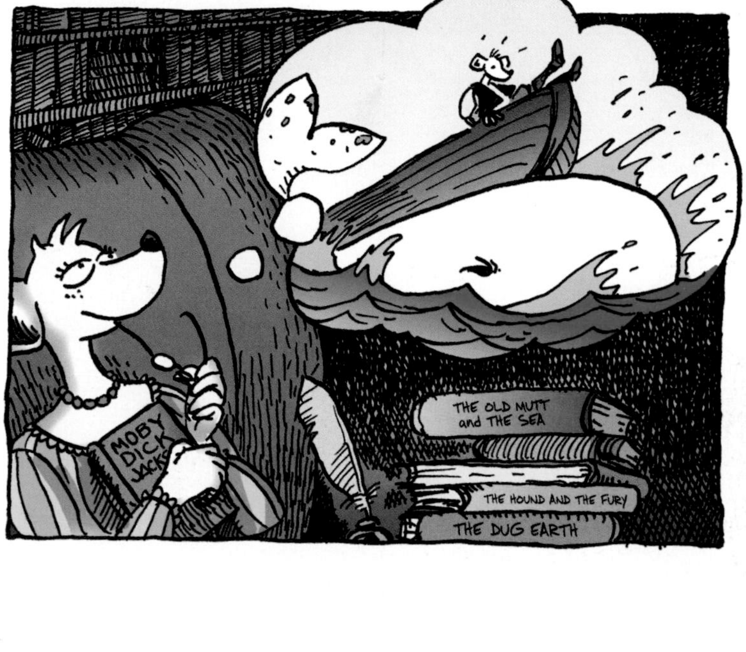
MOBY DICK
THE OLD MUTT and THE SEA
THE HOUND AND THE FURY
THE DUG EARTH

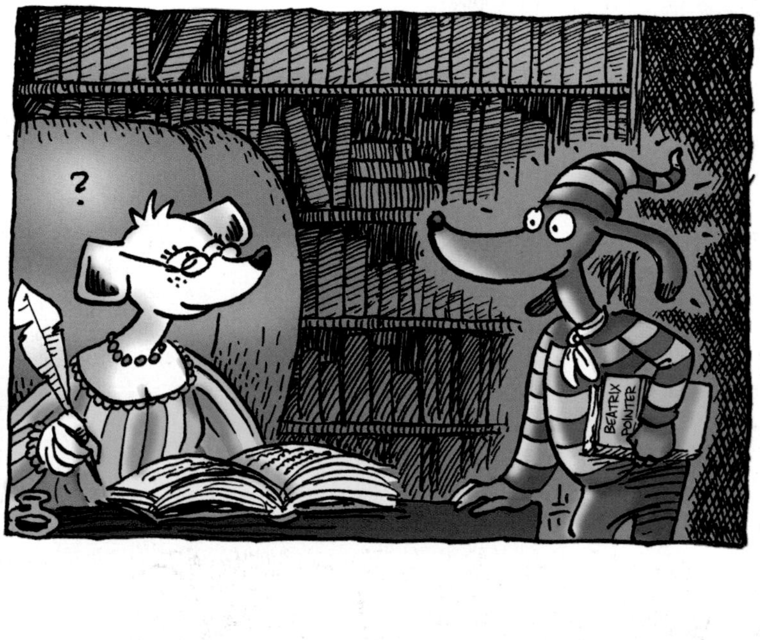
?
BEATRIX POINTER

The Wiener Dog

"Is it fair,"
Dear Dachshund whines,
"that I should do the cooking?
I know so many other tricks
those dogs are overlooking.
"It's always me
they send below
whene'er they want a nibble.
Doggone it! I am meant for more
than sausage links and kibble.
"I never dreamed
of serving snacks
out of a kitchen book.
Curse my luck, forever stuck—
a short, short-order cook."

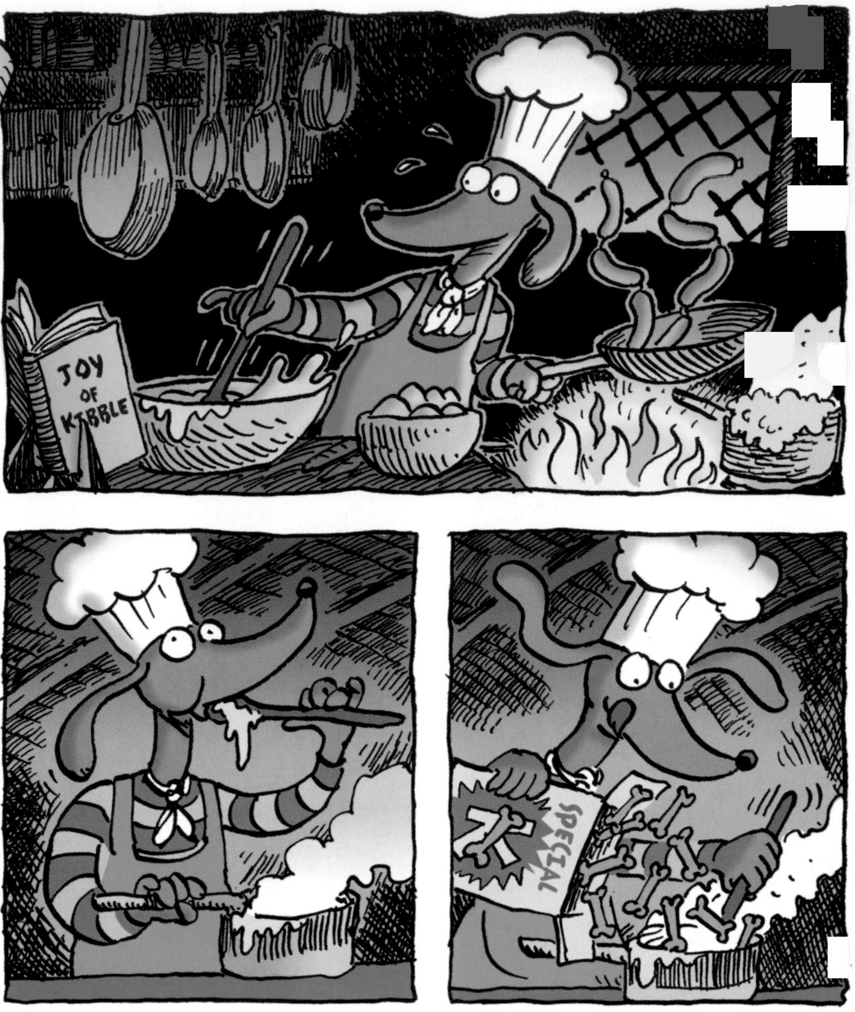
JOY OF KIBBLE
SPECIAL

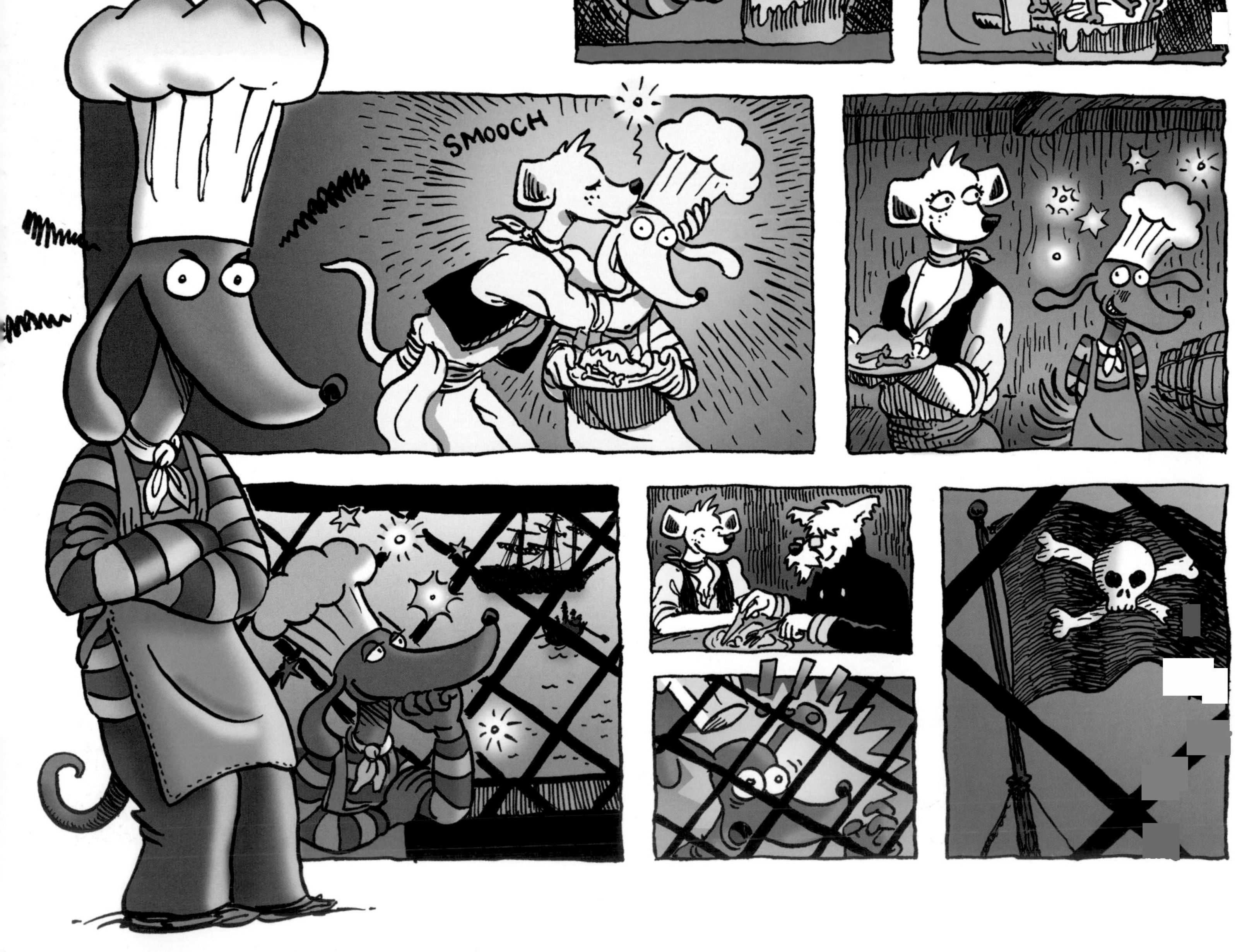
SMOOCH

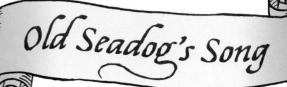

Old Seadog's Song

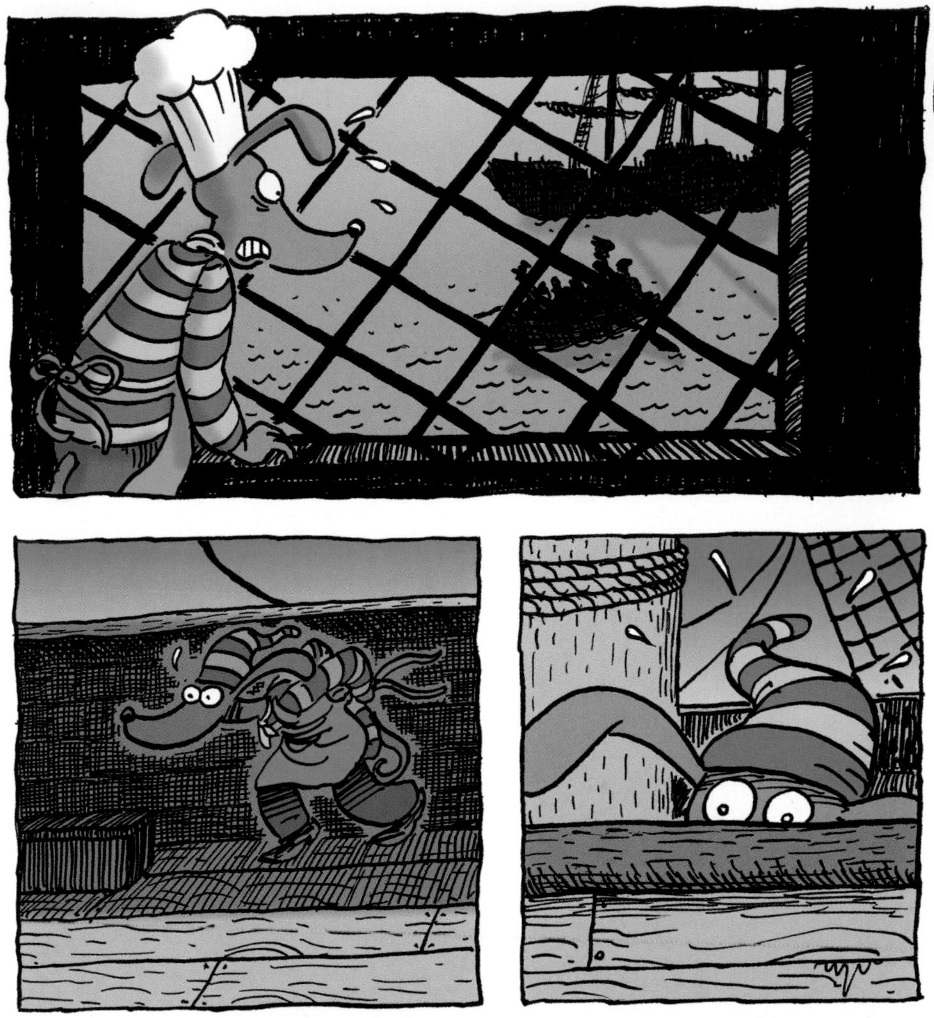

I met her in Dublin,
a fiery red lassie,
my Saltwater Taffy,
her life was the sea.

Her language was RUFF and
her manners were brassy.
Though I loved her faithful,
she cared not for me.

For she loved the ocean,
my Saltwater Taffy.
Her home was the ROVER,
her kin was its crew.

And I couldn't chain her,
that carefree young lassie.
She stole my poor heart,
then she nipped it in two.

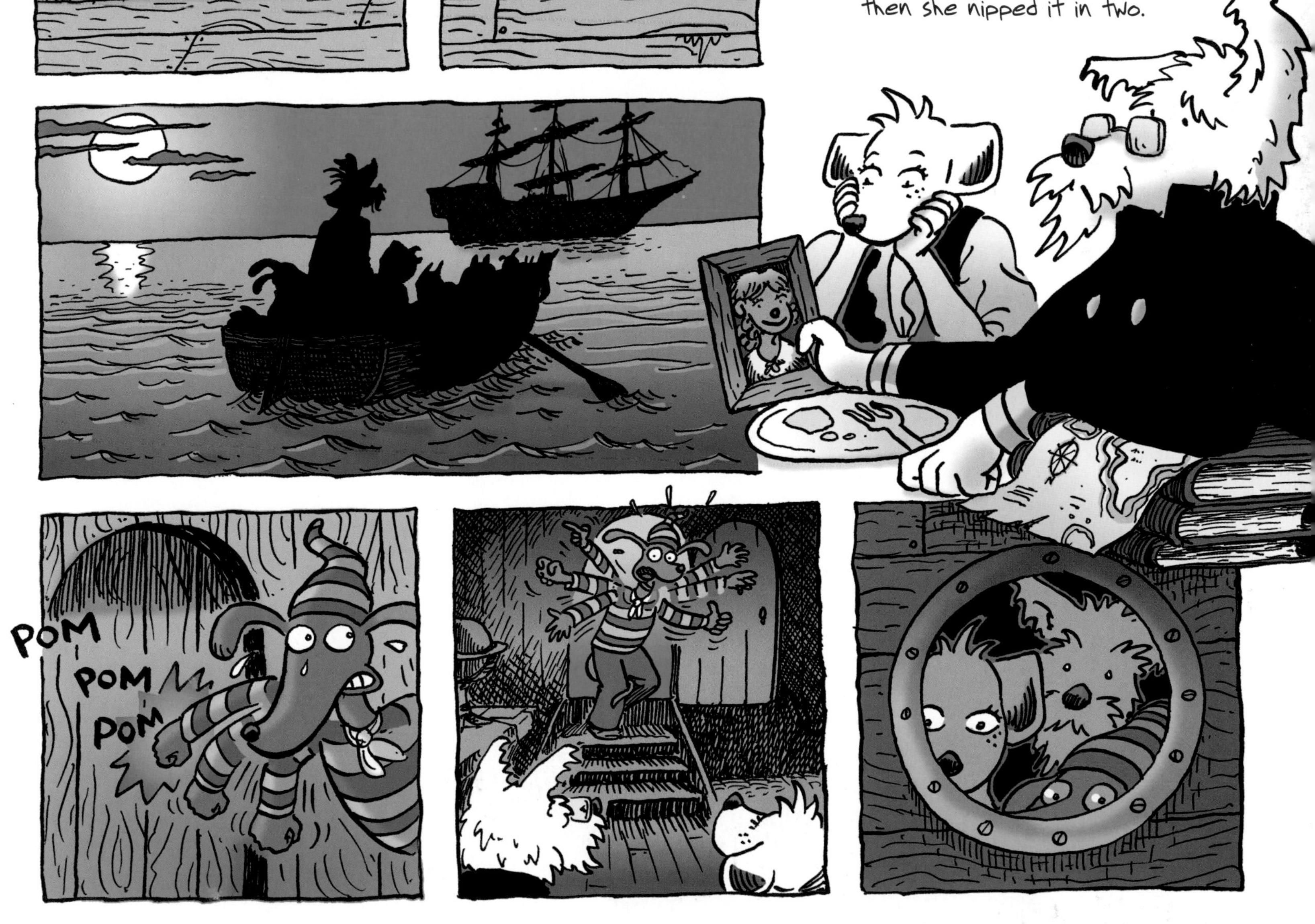
POM
POM
POM

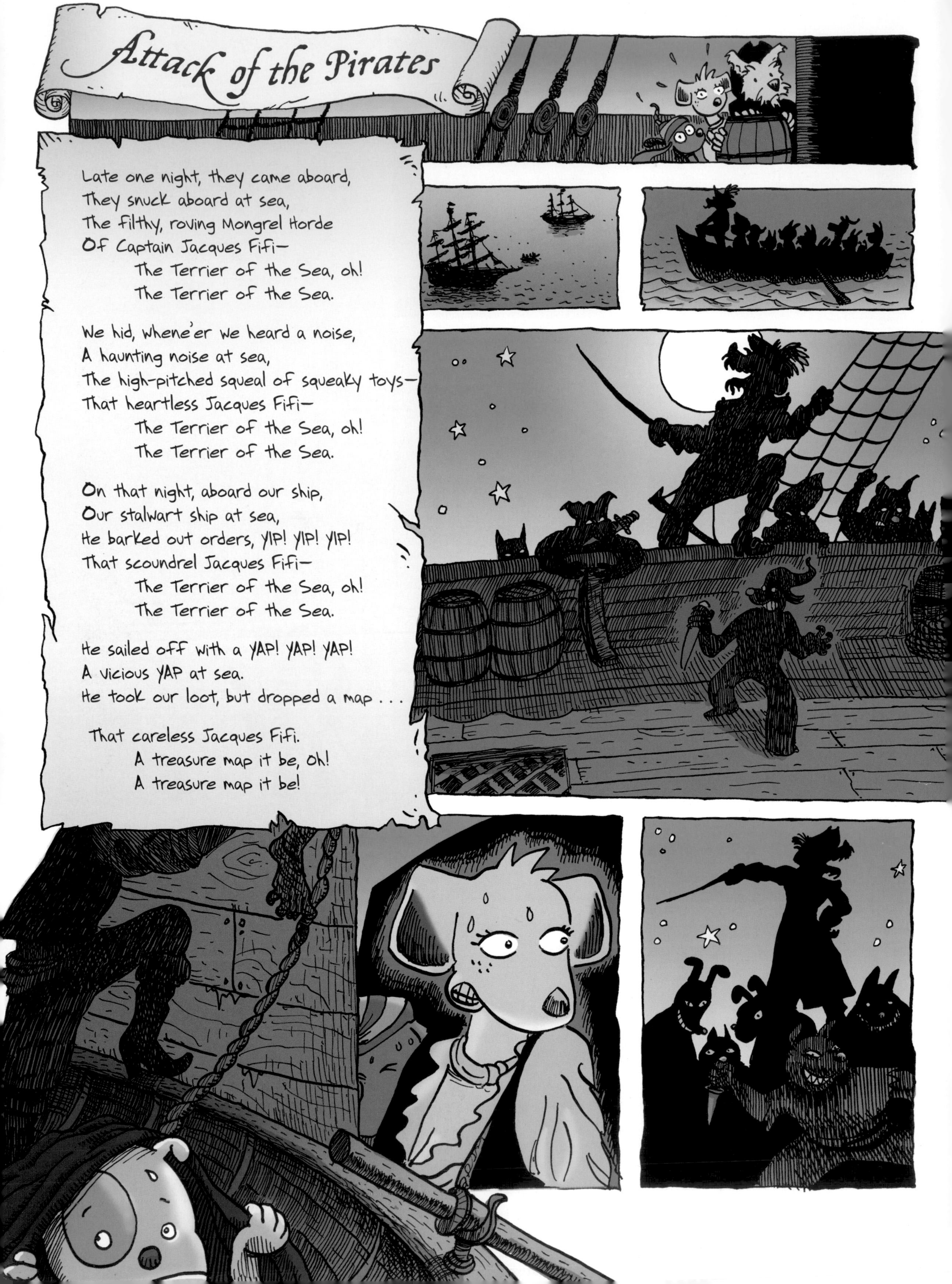
Attack of the Pirates
Late one night, they came aboard,
They snuck aboard at sea,
The filthy, roving Mongrel Horde
Of Captain Jacques Fifi—
The Terrier of the Sea, oh!
The Terrier of the Sea.
We hid, whene'er we heard a noise,
A haunting noise at sea,
The high-pitched squeal of squeaky toys—
That heartless Jacques Fifi—
The Terrier of the Sea, oh!
The Terrier of the Sea.
On that night, aboard our ship,
Our stalwart ship at sea,
He barked out orders, YIP! YIP! YIP!
That scoundrel Jacques Fifi—
The Terrier of the Sea, oh!
The Terrier of the Sea.
He sailed off with a YAP! YAP! YAP!
A vicious YAP at sea.
He took our loot, but dropped a map . . .
That careless Jacques Fifi.
A treasure map it be, oh!
A treasure map it be!

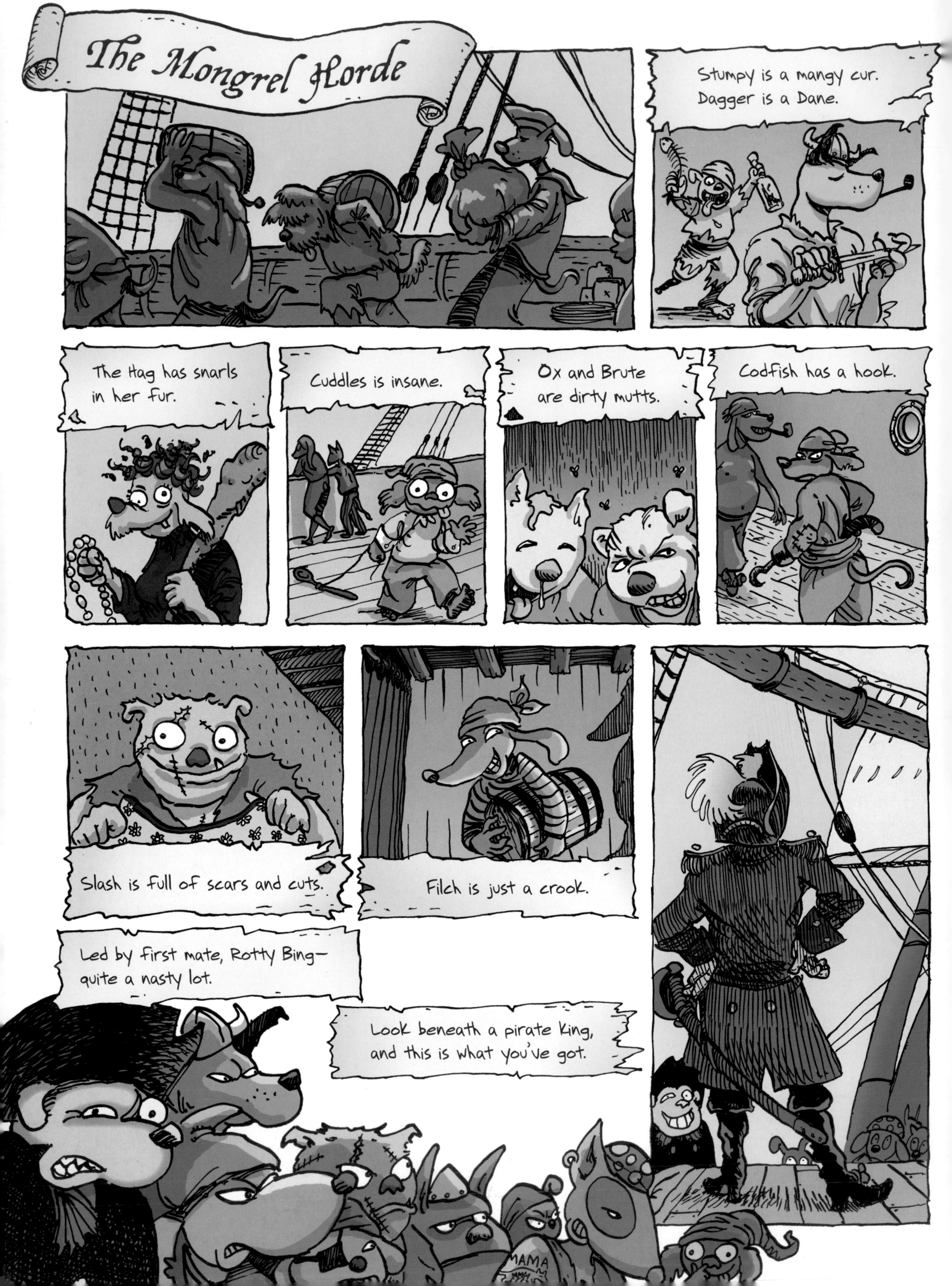
The Mongrel Horde
Stumpy is a mangy cur.
Dagger is a Dane.
The Hag has snarls in her fur.
Cuddles is insane.
Ox and Brute are dirty mutts.
Codfish has a hook.
Slash is full of scars and cuts.
Filch is just a crook.
Led by first mate, Rotty Bing—quite a nasty lot.
Look beneath a pirate king, and this is what you've got.
MAMA

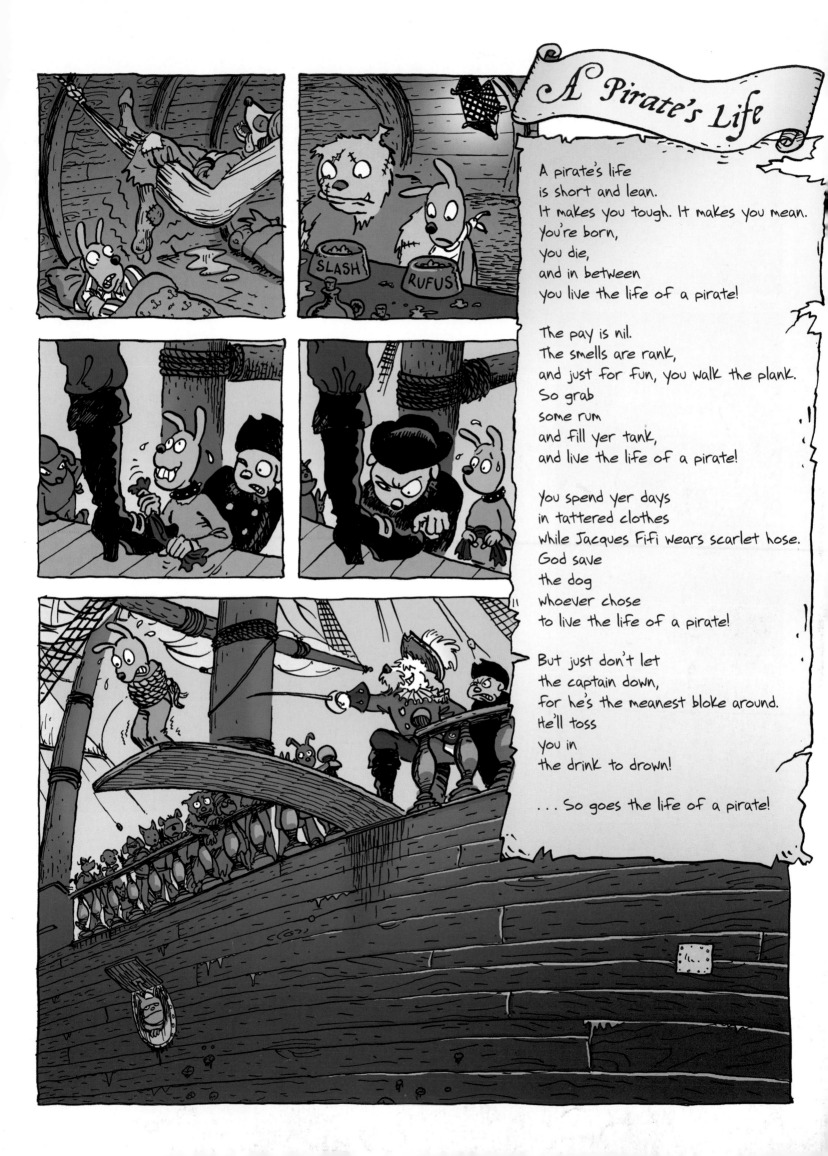

A Pirate's Life

A pirate's life
is short and lean.
It makes you tough. It makes you mean.
You're born,
you die,
and in between
you live the life of a pirate!

The pay is nil.
The smells are rank,
and just for fun, you walk the plank.
So grab
some rum
and fill yer tank,
and live the life of a pirate!

You spend yer days
in tattered clothes
while Jacques Fifi wears scarlet hose.
God save
the dog
whoever chose
to live the life of a pirate!

But just don't let
the captain down,
for he's the meanest bloke around.
He'll toss
you in
the drink to drown!

. . . So goes the life of a pirate!

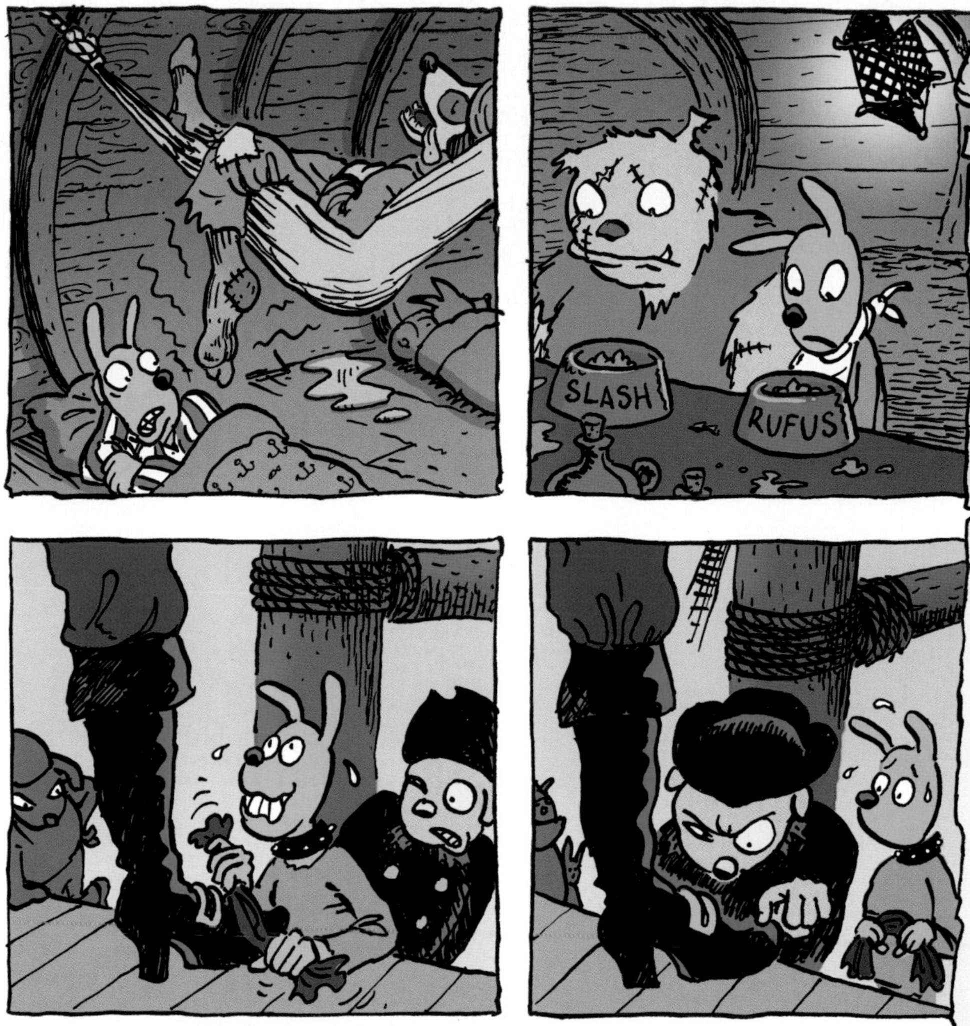
SLASH
RUFUS

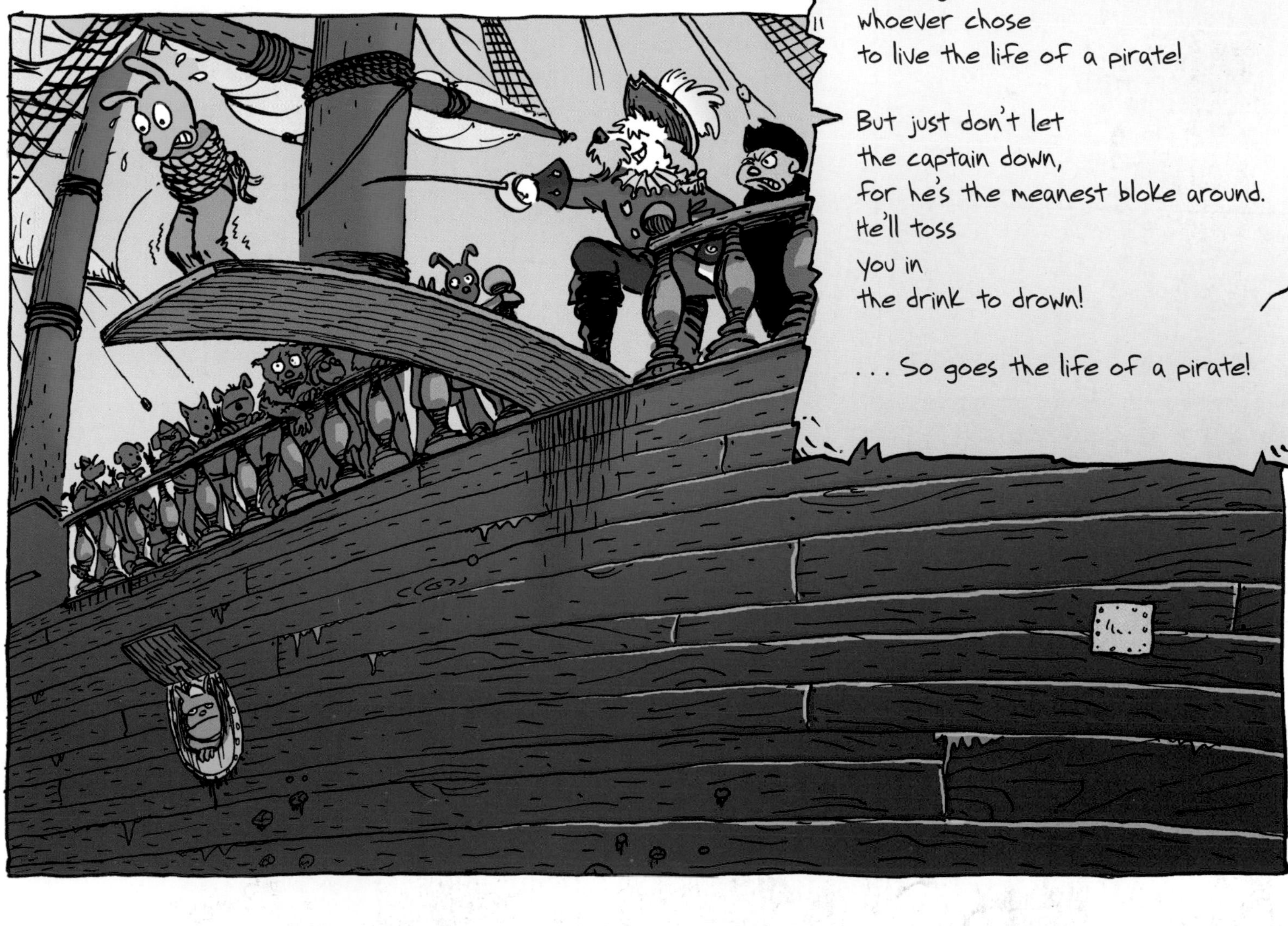

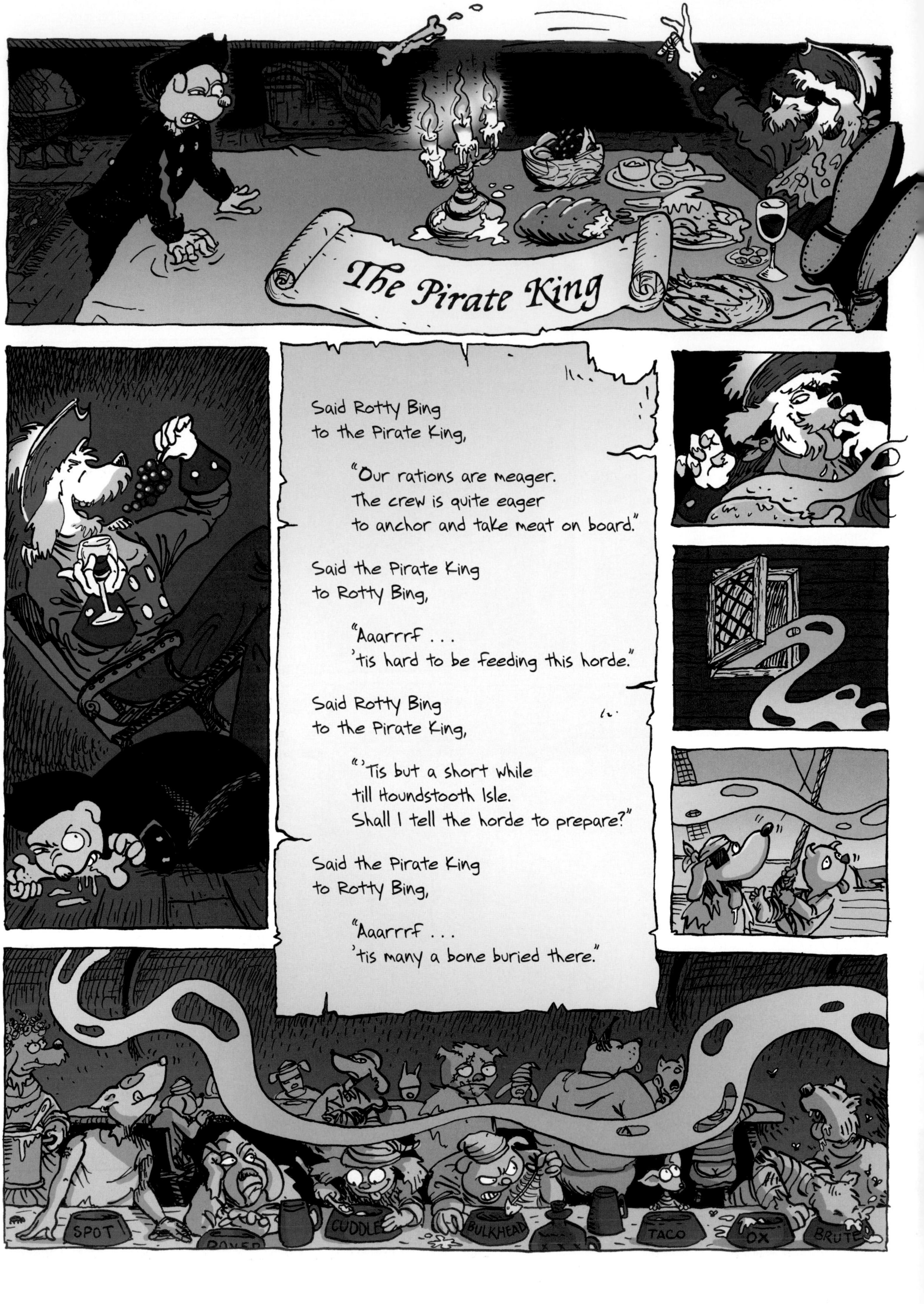
The Pirate King
Said Rotty Bing
to the Pirate King,
"Our rations are meager.
The crew is quite eager
to anchor and take meat on board."
Said the Pirate King
to Rotty Bing,
"Aaarrrf . . .
'tis hard to be feeding this horde."
Said Rotty Bing
to the Pirate King,
"'Tis but a short while
till Houndstooth Isle.
Shall I tell the horde to prepare?"
Said the Pirate King
to Rotty Bing,
"Aaarrrf . . .
'tis many a bone buried there."
SPOT
CUDDLE
BULKHEAD
TACO
OX
BRUTE

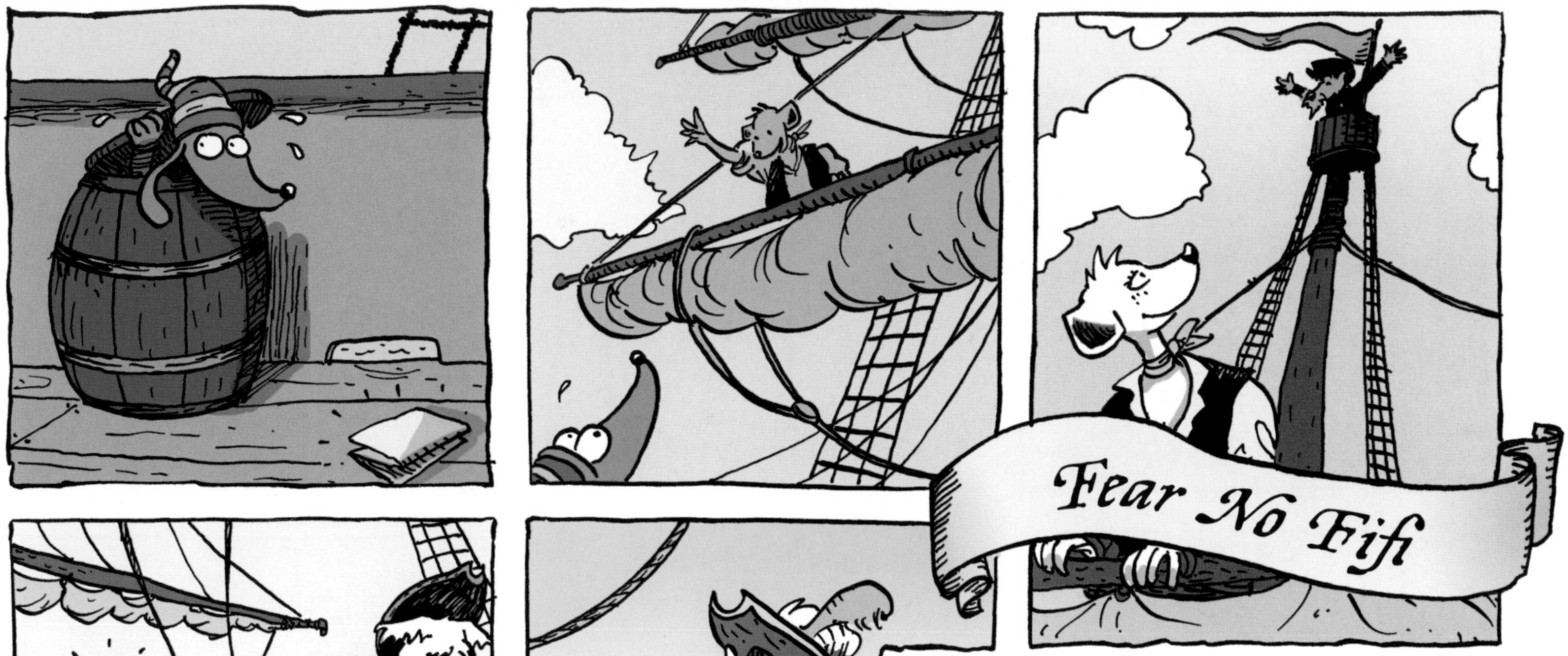
Fear No Fifi

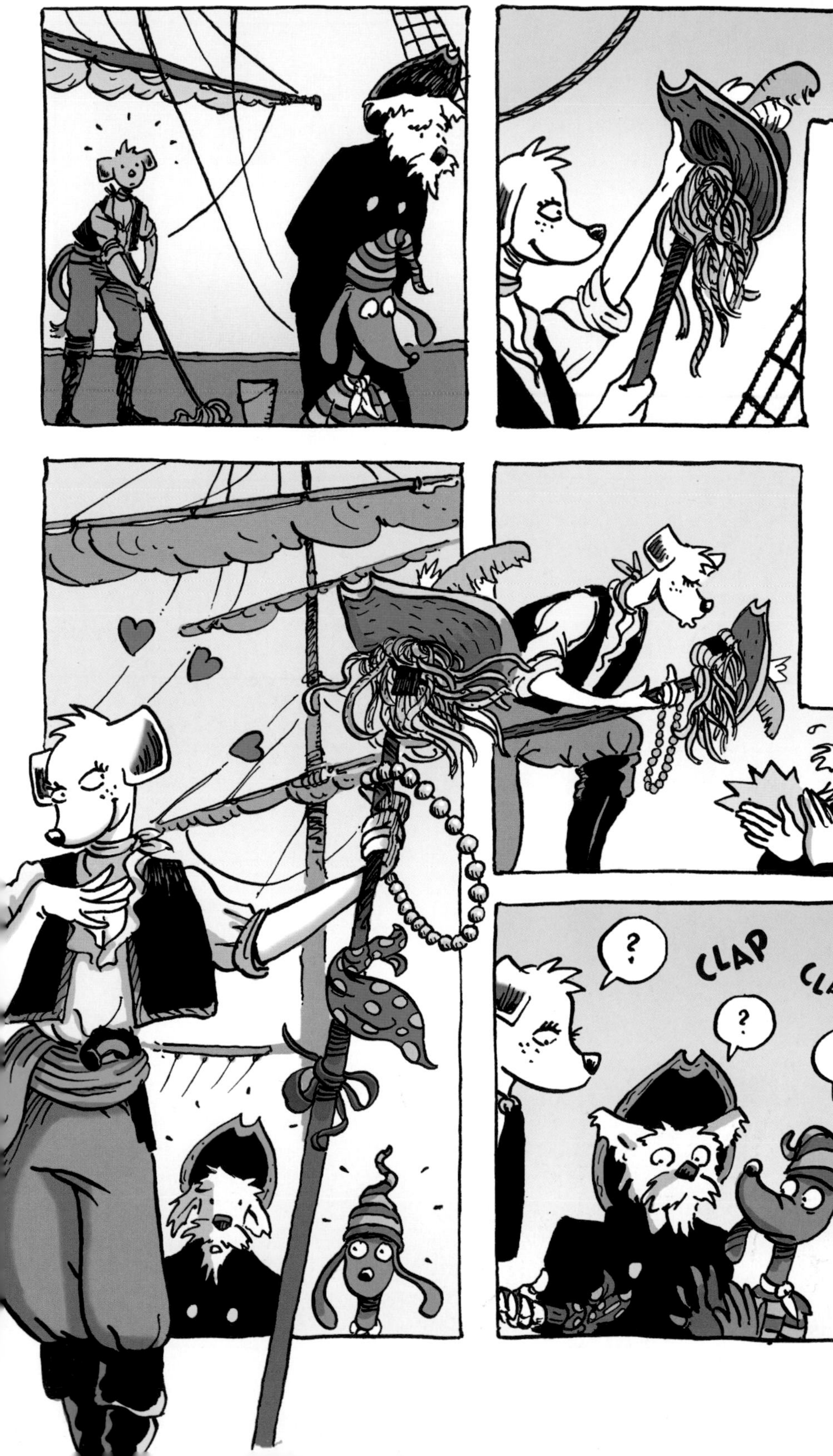

The Pirate King wears fancy clothes.
A silver ring adorns his nose.
A private groomer paints his toes—
each nail is brushed with gold.

His collar's set with precious stones.
He dabs his fur with rare colognes.
He dines on choice and savory bones
. . . or so I have been told.

Oh, why do houndsome hearts grow faint
at pirates decked in pearls and paint?
If he's a threat, then I'm a saint
. . . a wonder to behold!

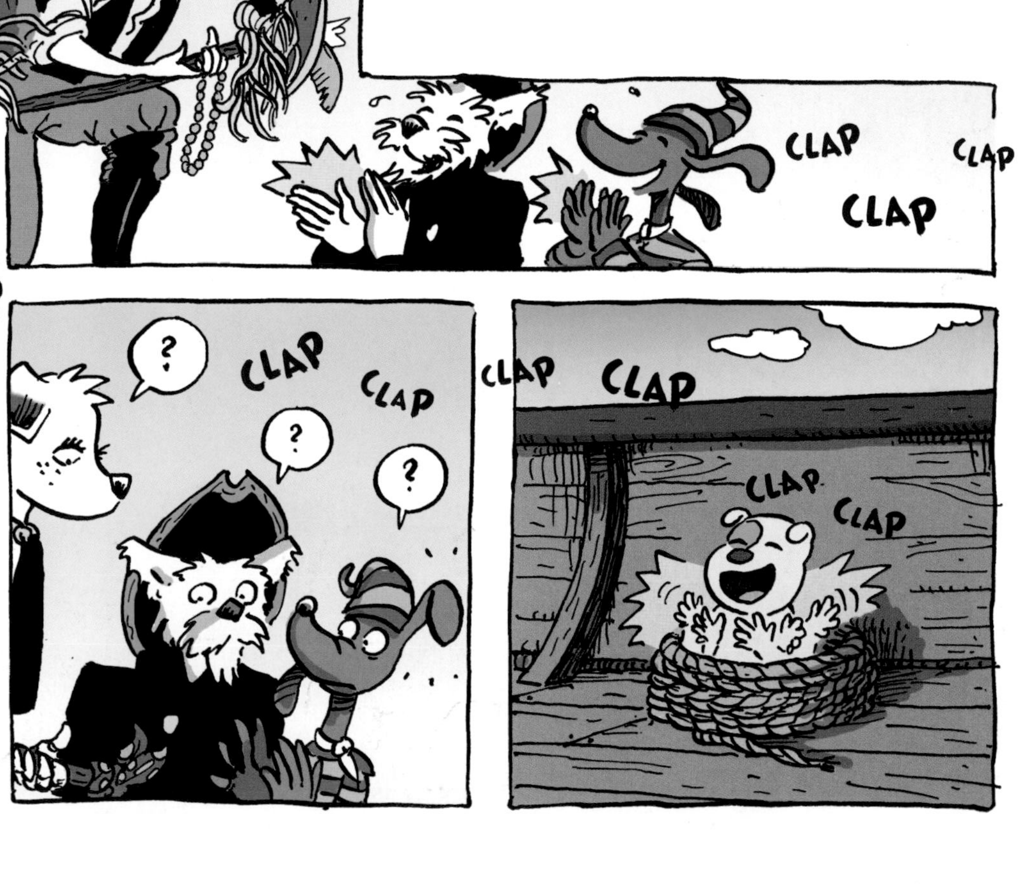
CLAP
CLAP
CLAP
?
CLAP
CLAP
?
?
CLAP
CLAP
CLAP
CLAP

The Stowaway

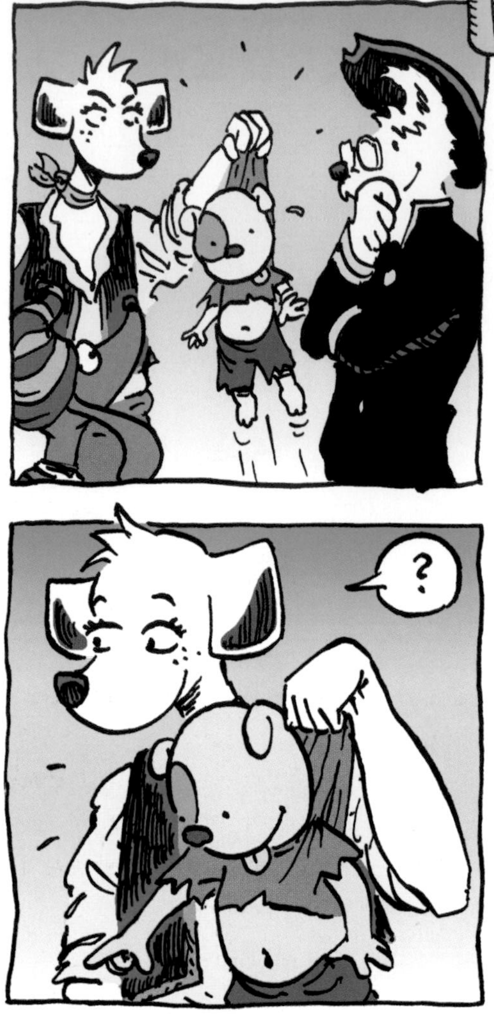

?

On the poop deck,
halfway hidden,
Beagle found a
wee, young pup.

"Looky here—
a cabin boy!"
She snatched his scruff
and scooped him up.

"What to do
with flea-bit beggars?
Should we toss him
in the drink?"

Old Seadog scratched
his brindled whiskers.
"This pup needs a home,
I think."

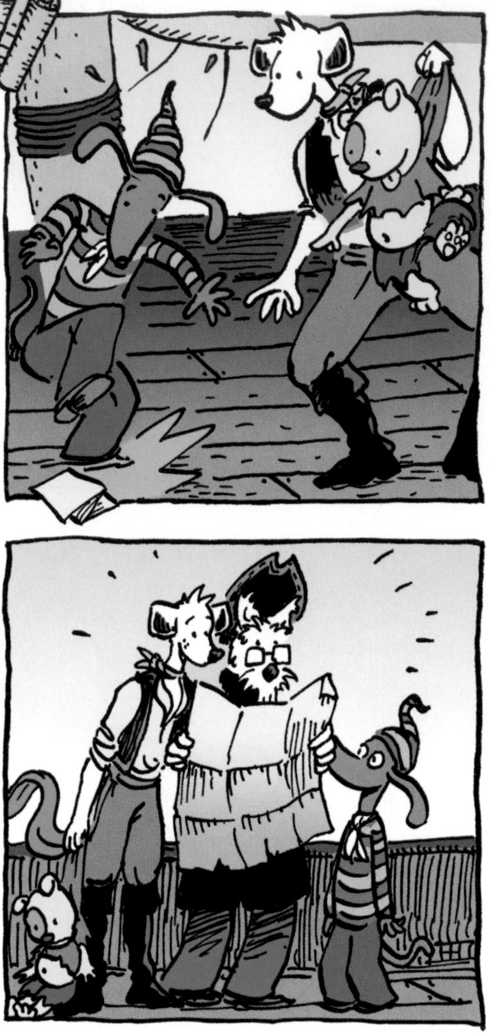

Follow the Map

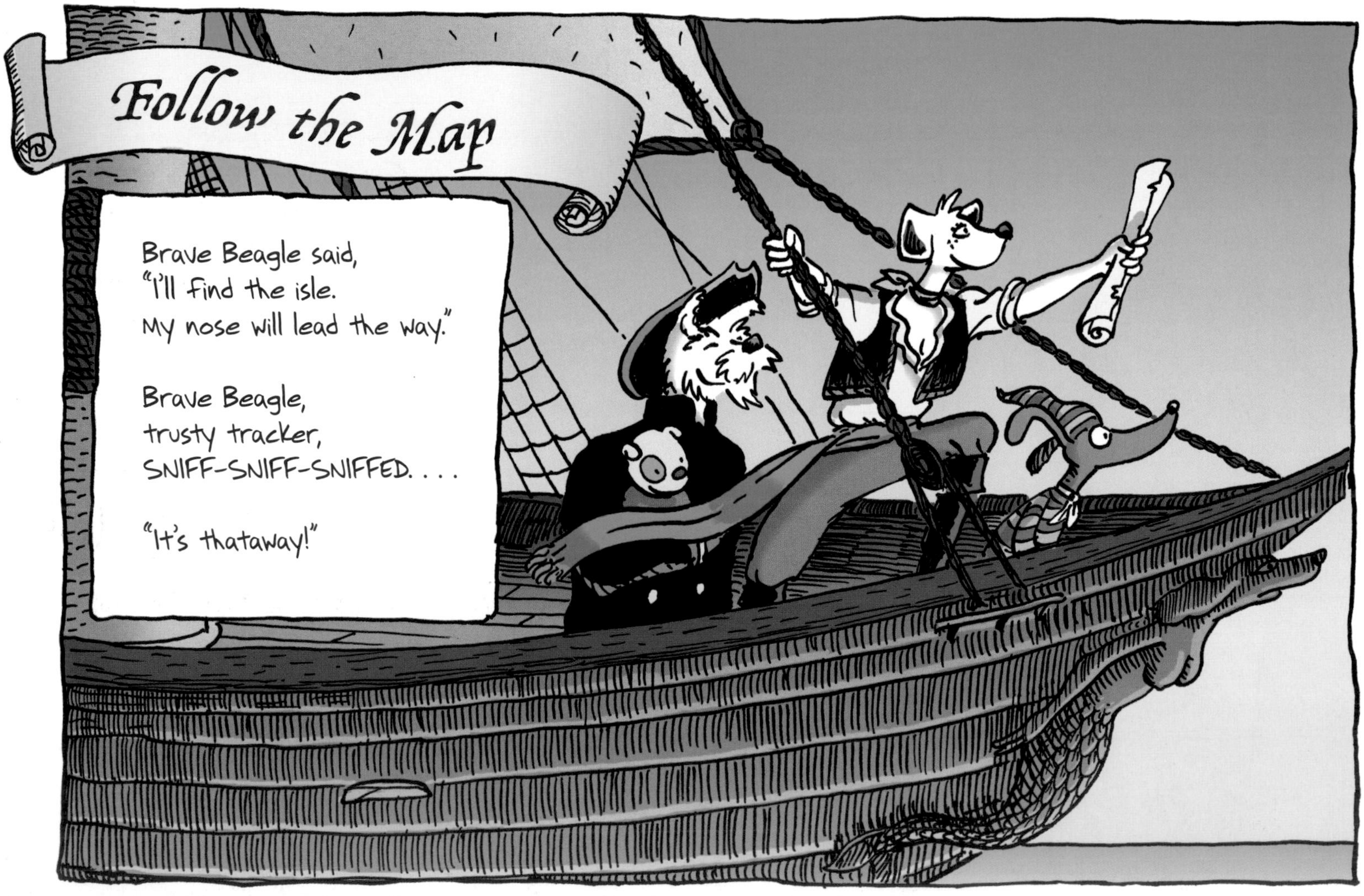

Brave Beagle said,
"I'll find the isle.
My nose will lead the way."

Brave Beagle,
trusty tracker,
SNIFF-SNIFF-SNIFFED. . . .

"It's thataway!"

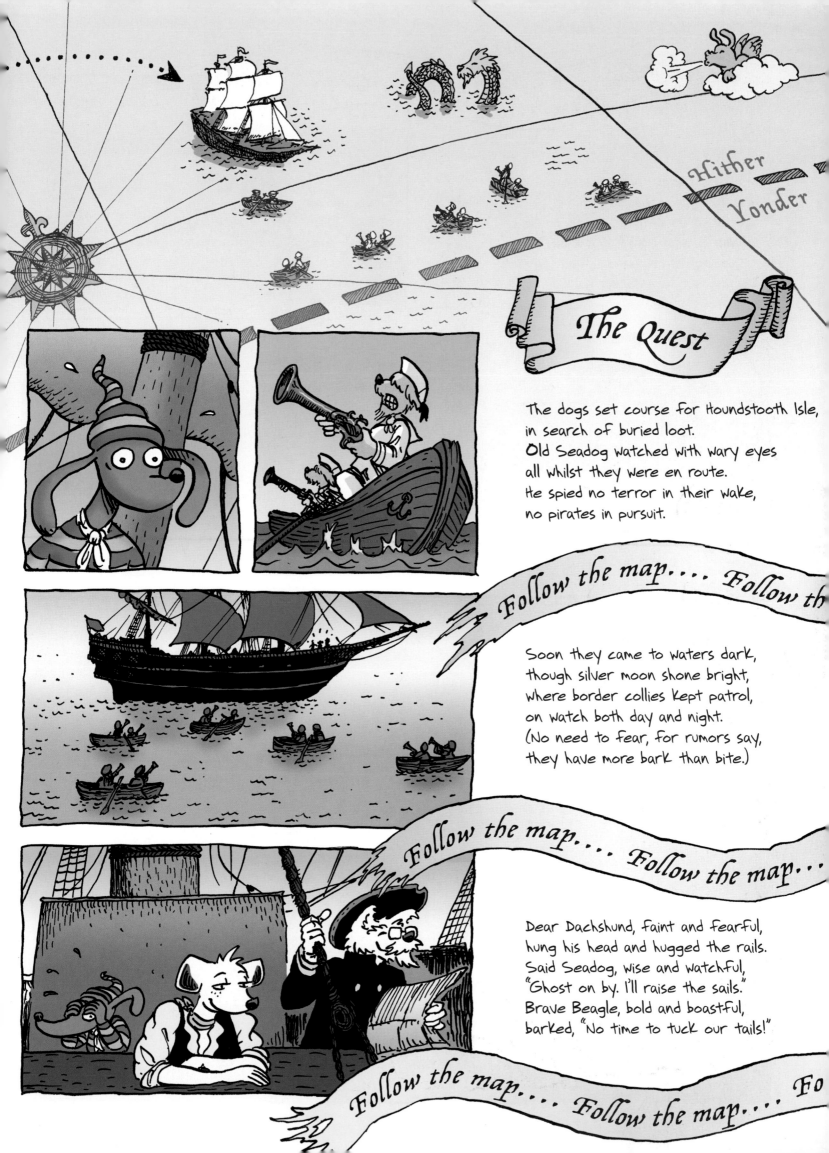

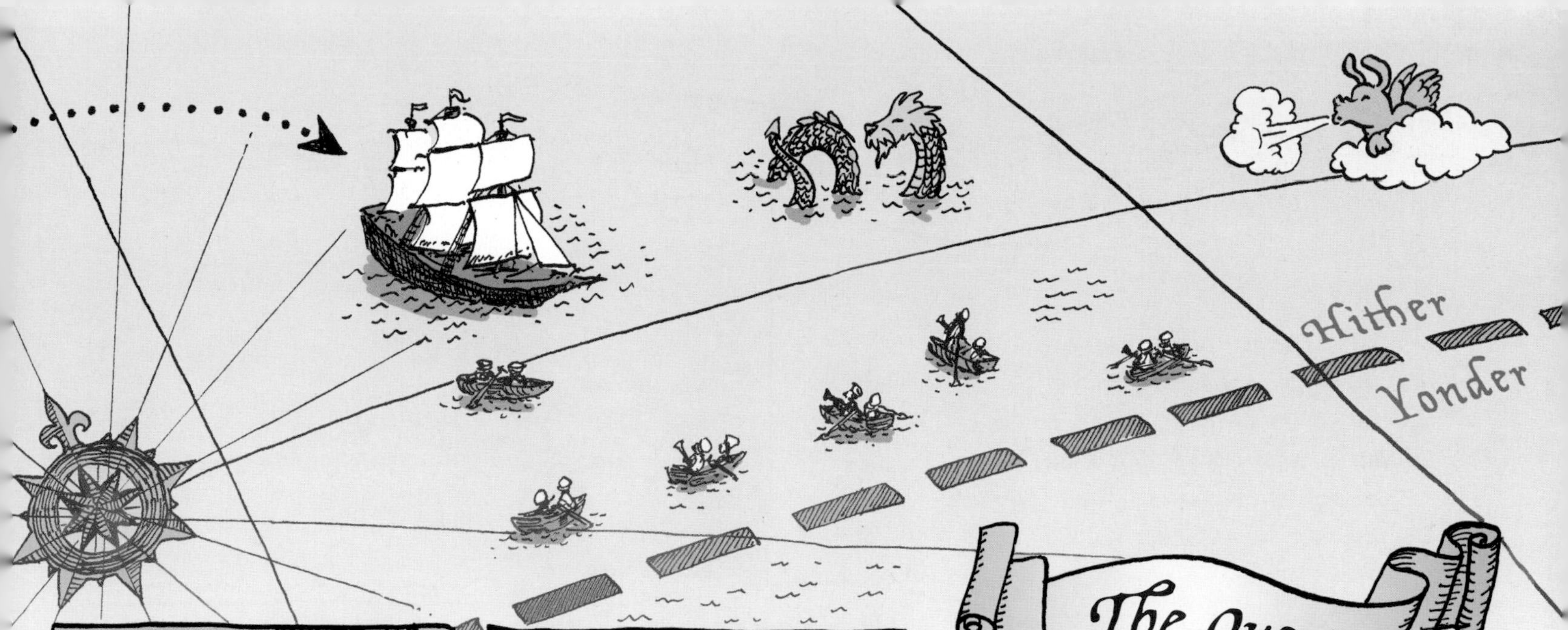
Hither
Yonder

The Quest

The dogs set course for Houndstooth Isle,
in search of buried loot.
Old Seadog watched with wary eyes
all whilst they were en route.
He spied no terror in their wake,
no pirates in pursuit.

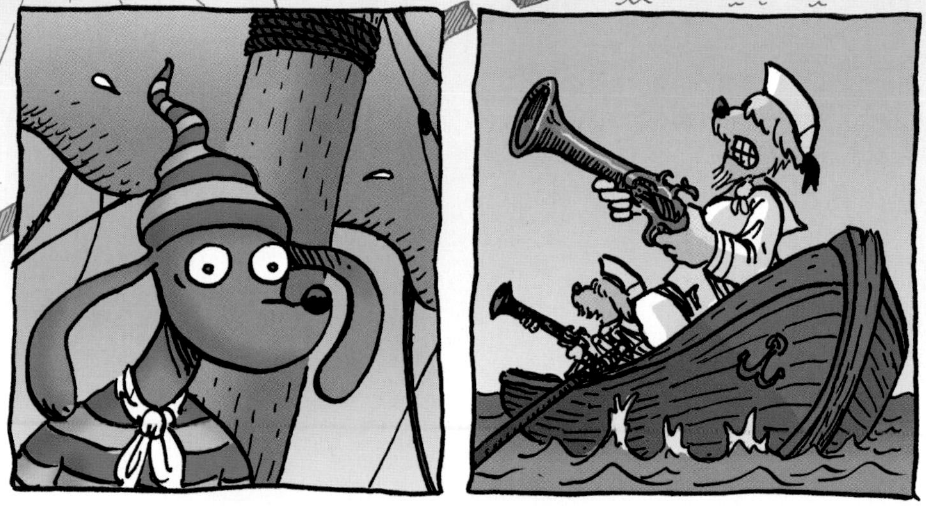

Follow the map.... Follow th

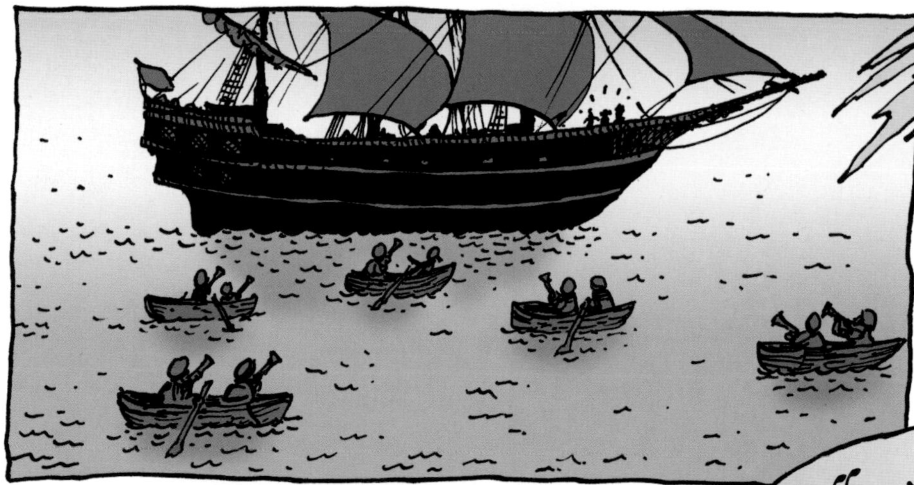

Soon they came to waters dark,
though silver moon shone bright,
where border collies kept patrol,
on watch both day and night.
(No need to fear, for rumors say,
they have more bark than bite.)

Follow the map.... Follow the map...

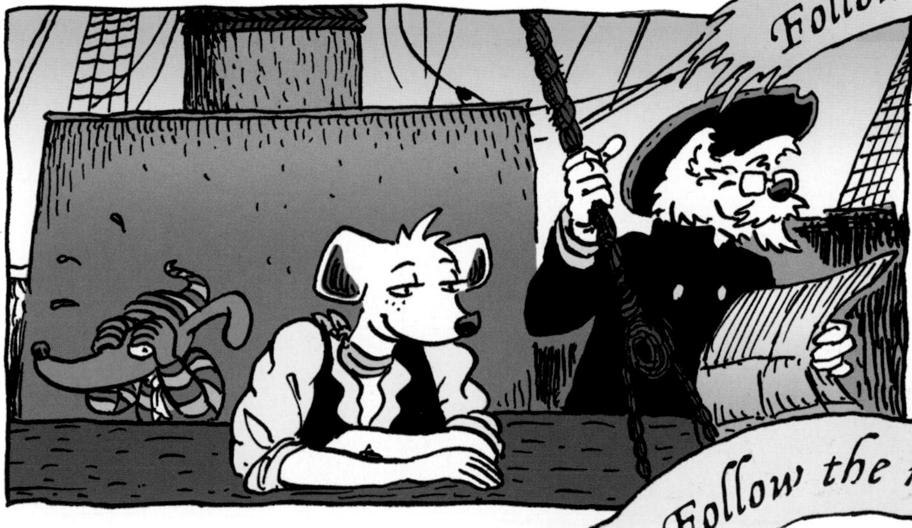

Dear Dachshund, faint and fearful,
hung his head and hugged the rails.
Said Seadog, wise and watchful,
"Ghost on by. I'll raise the sails."
Brave Beagle, bold and boastful,
barked, "No time to tuck our tails!"

Follow the map.... Follow the map.... Fo

the map.... Follow the map.... Follow the map.

They sailed on past the border
in a hail of howls and barks.
They sailed on past those collies
midst a swarm of hungry sharks.
They sailed on toward their destiny—
a map with crossbone marks.

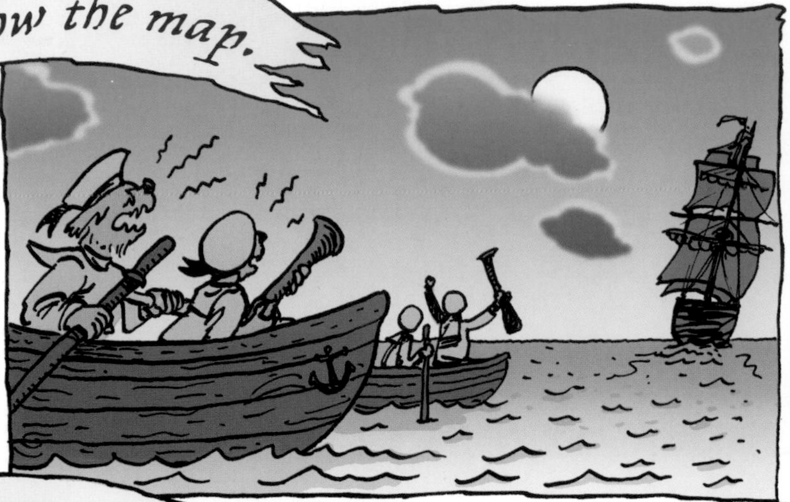

Follow the map.... Follow the map.... Follow th

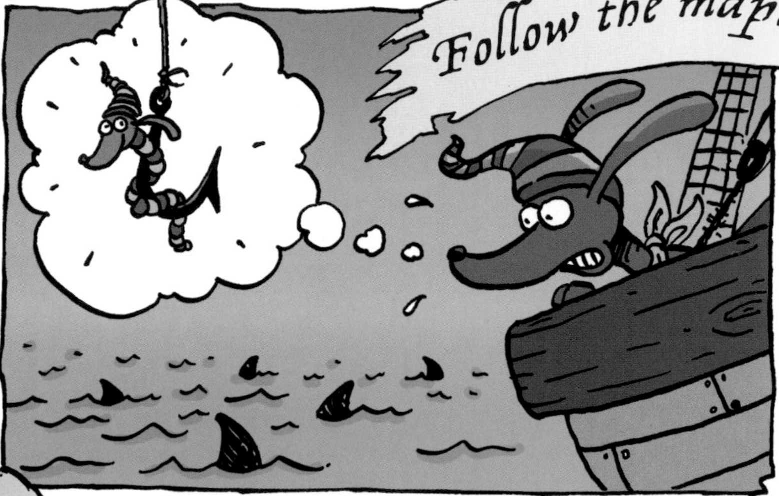

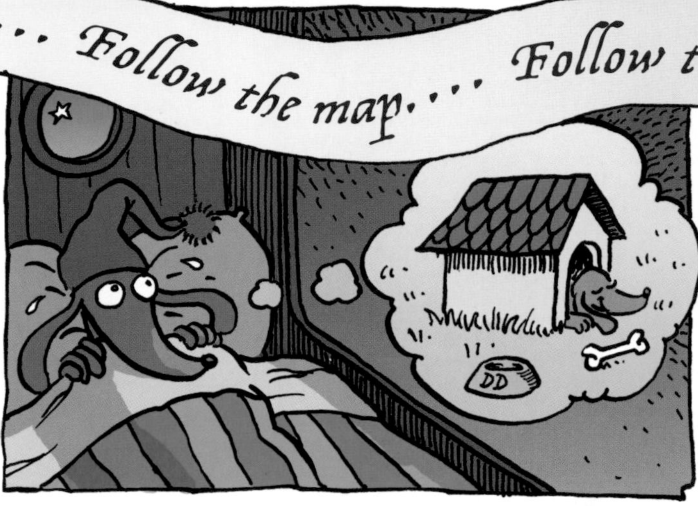

Pup's Lullaby

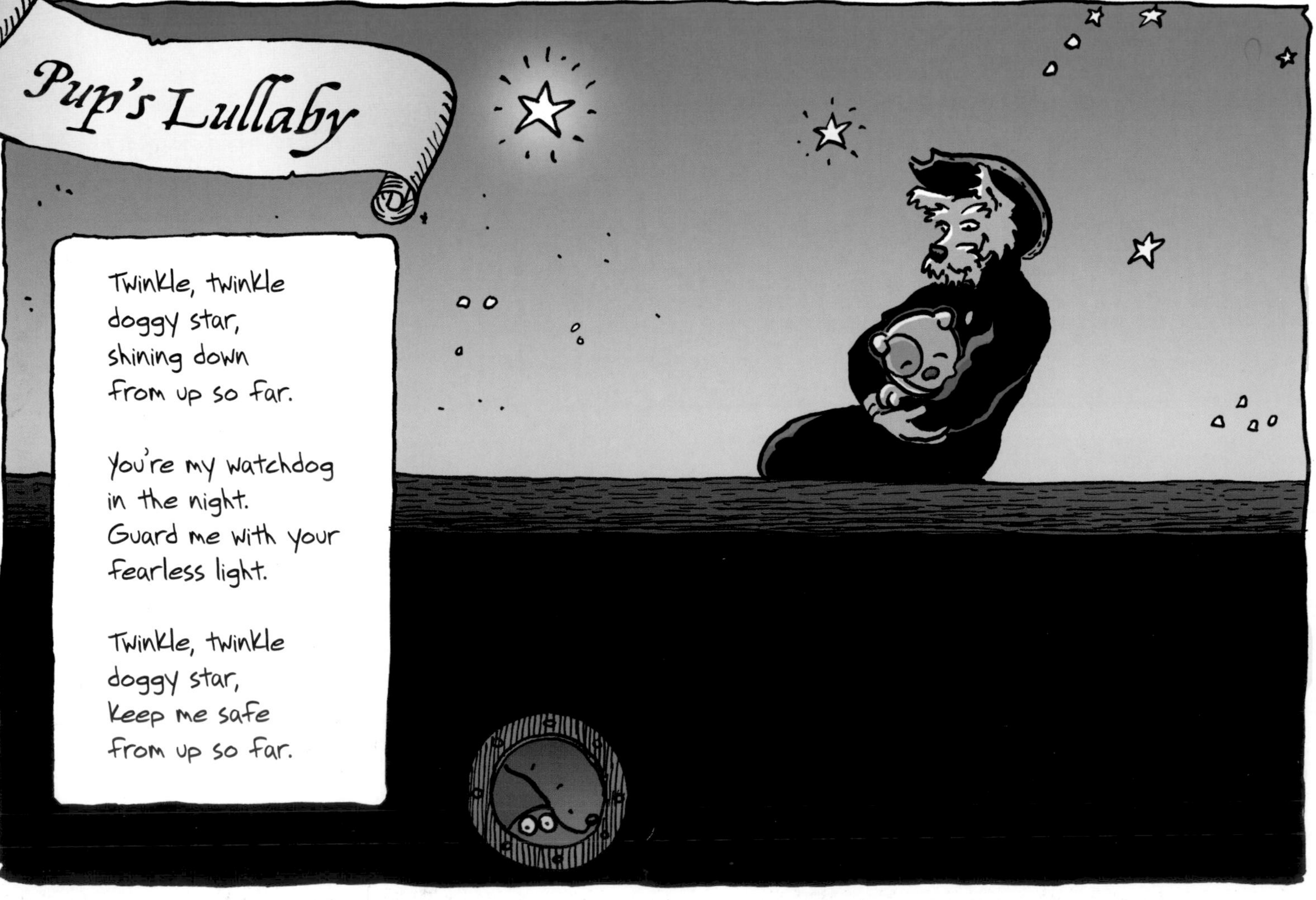

Twinkle, twinkle
doggy star,
shining down
from up so far.

You're my watchdog
in the night.
Guard me with your
fearless light.

Twinkle, twinkle
doggy star,
keep me safe
from up so far.

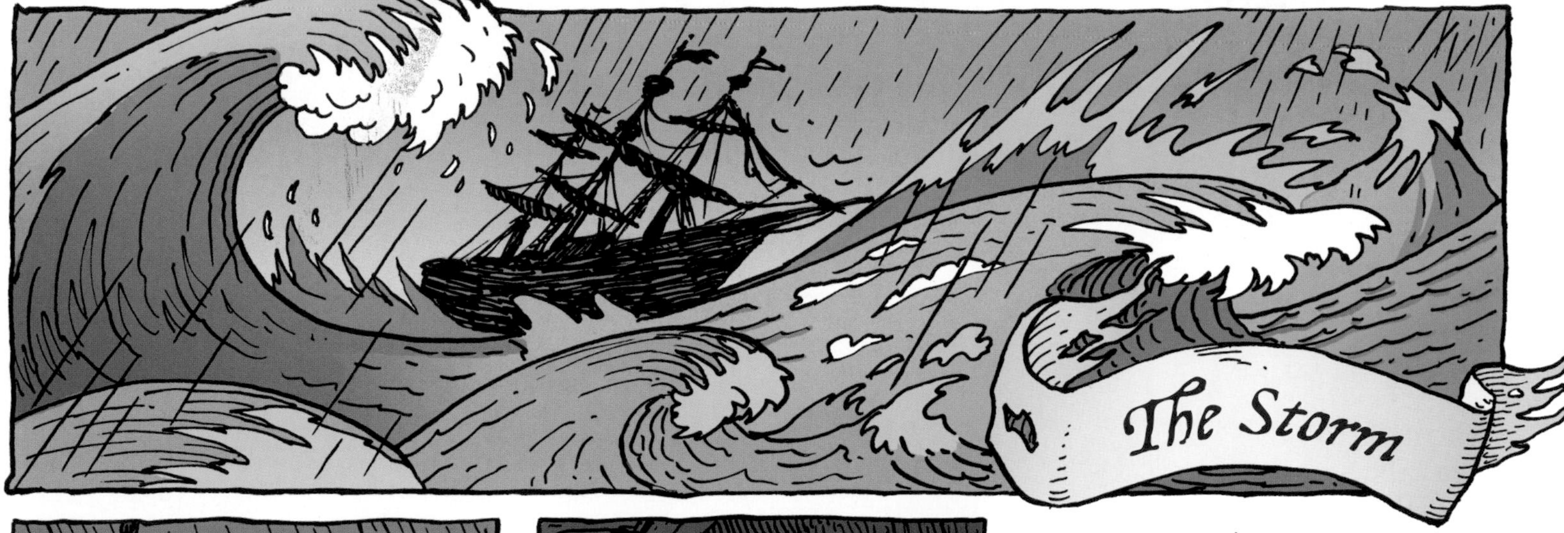
The Storm

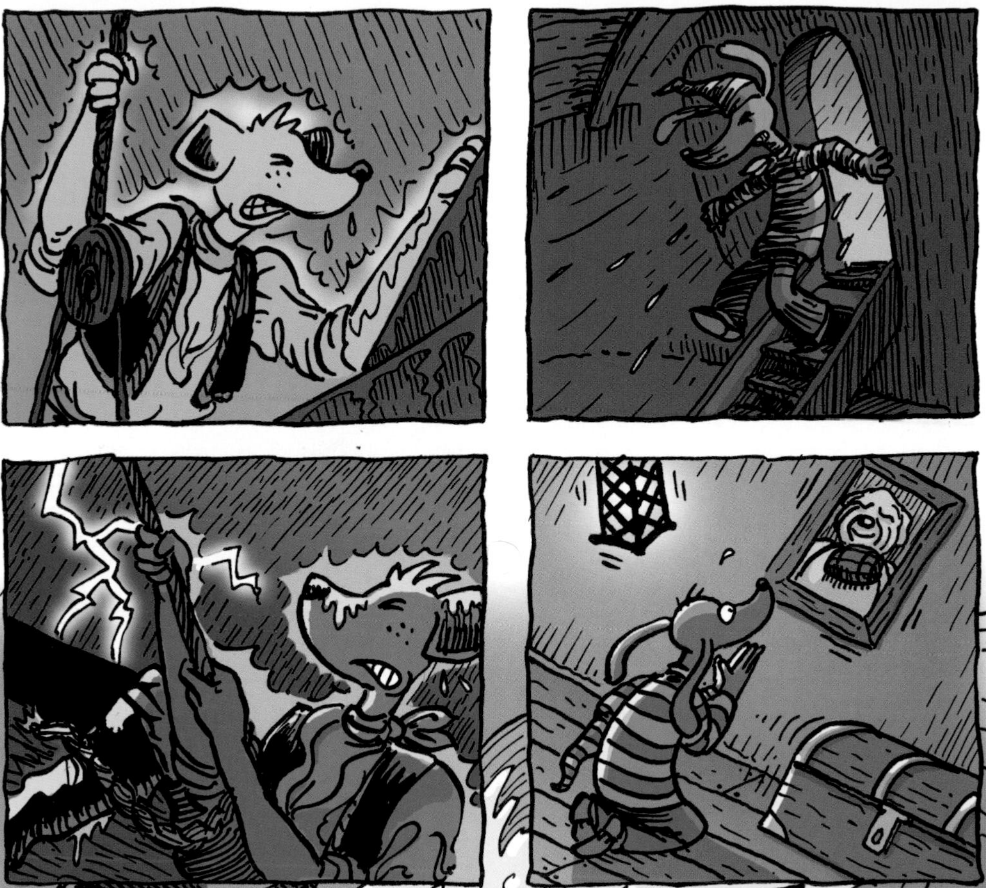

A sudden gale,
with pounding hail,
hit just beyond the coast.
Brave Beagle howled
within the storm,
but never left her post.

Raindrops lashed,
as lightning flashed,
the wind whipped cold and hard.
Dear Dachshund dropped
on trembling knees
and prayed to Saint Bernard.

Old Seadog, true,
knew what to do,
he led his crew with style.
All through the night
he chose to fight:
"Onward! Houndstooth Isle!"

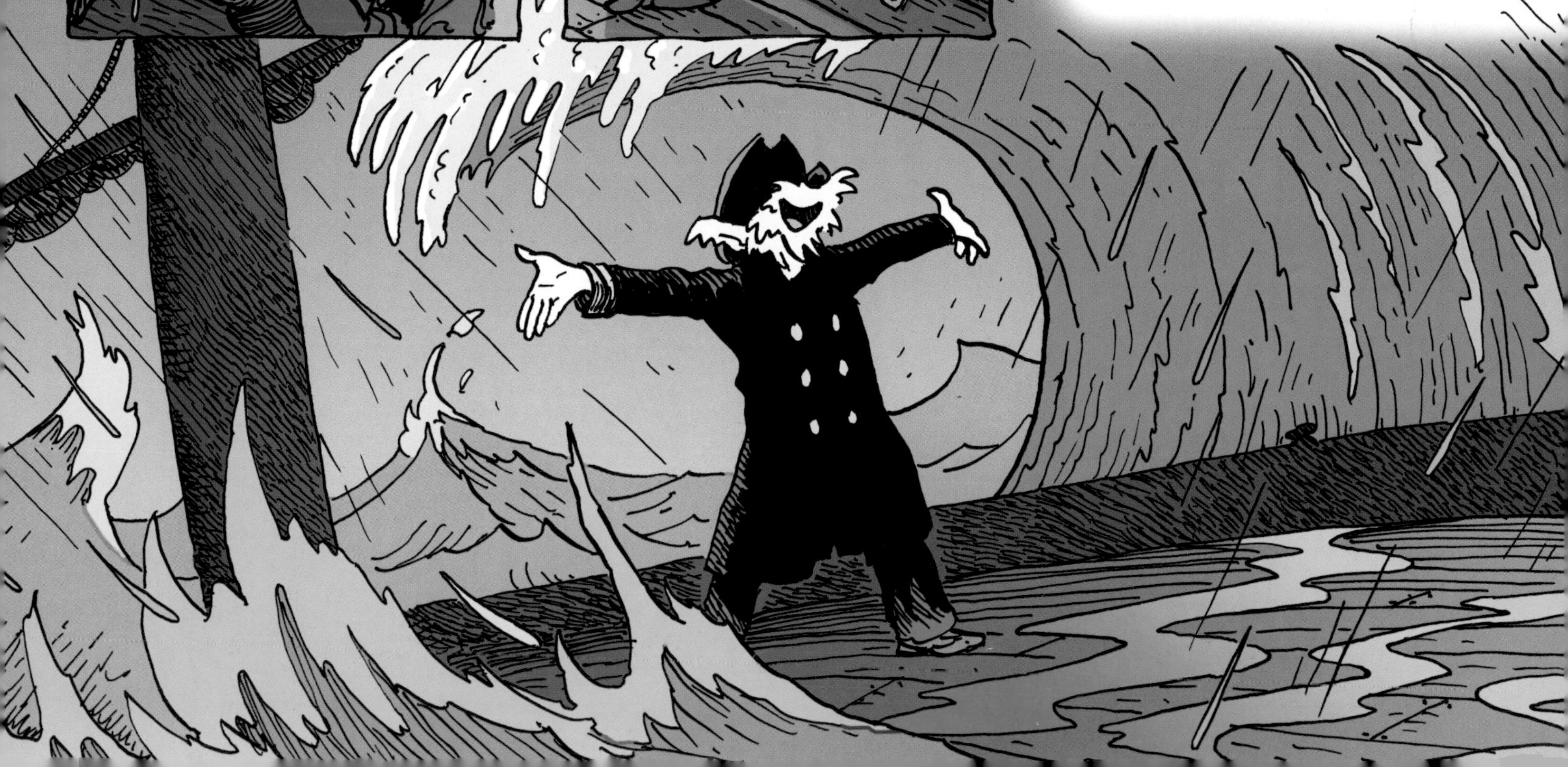

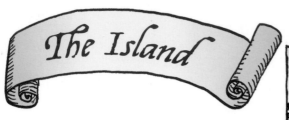

The Island

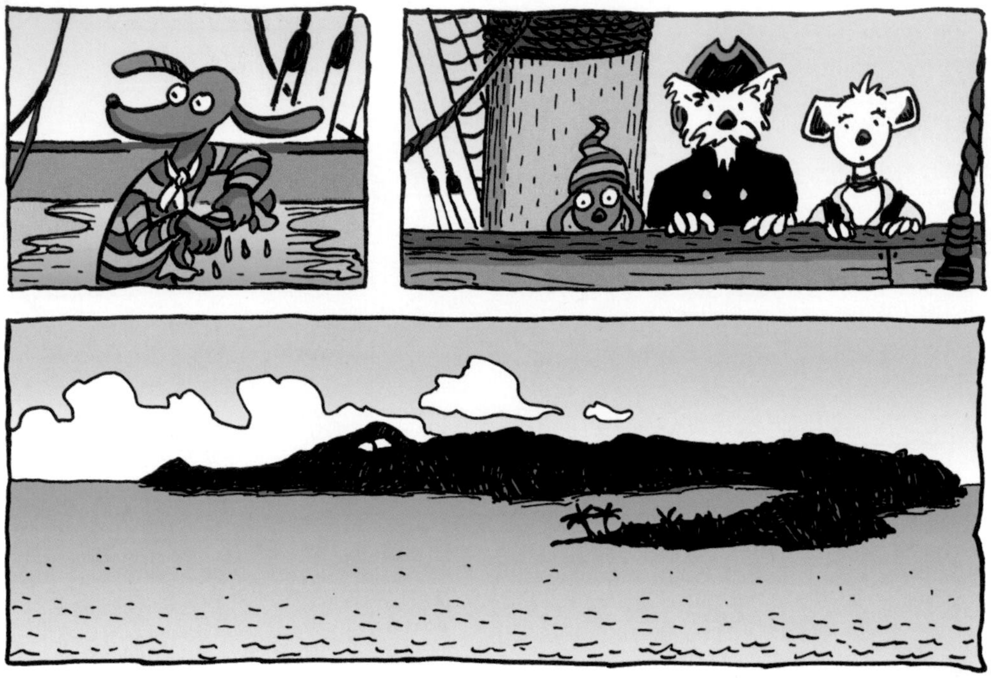

Like a shadow on the water,
like a croc upon the Nile,
it lies waiting
poised and patient —
a foreboding, fateful isle.

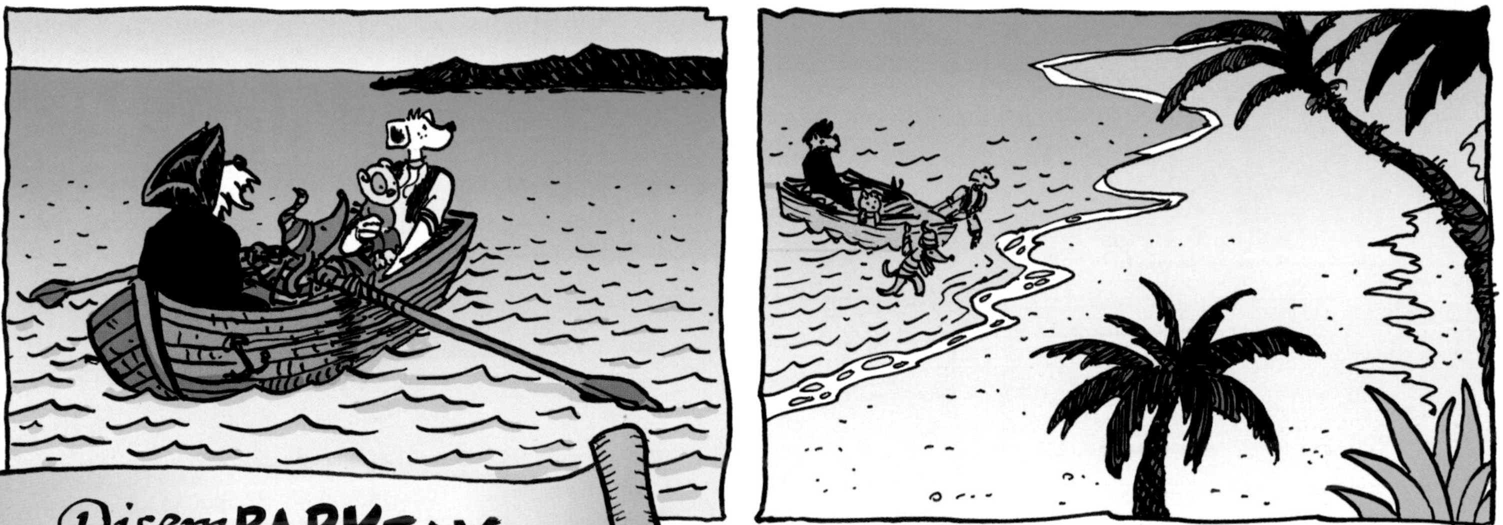

DisemBARKING

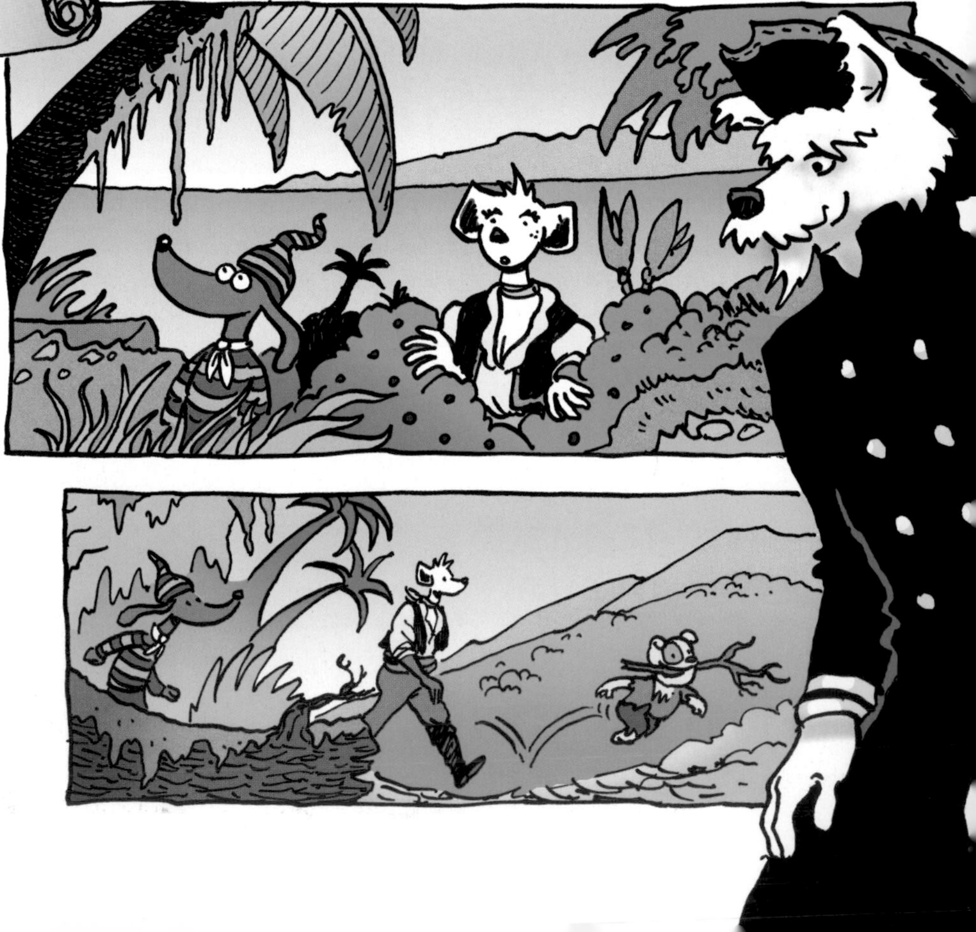

Dogs set paws upon the sand.
Now Old Seadog takes command,
barking orders to his crew.

"FETCH!" RUFF! RUFF!
"JUMP!" WOOF! WOOF!
"STAY!" ARF! ARF!
"SPEAK!" AARROOOOOOOO!

As he barks, the honest pup
smiles and says, "When I grow up,
I want to be just like **YOOOOOOO**."

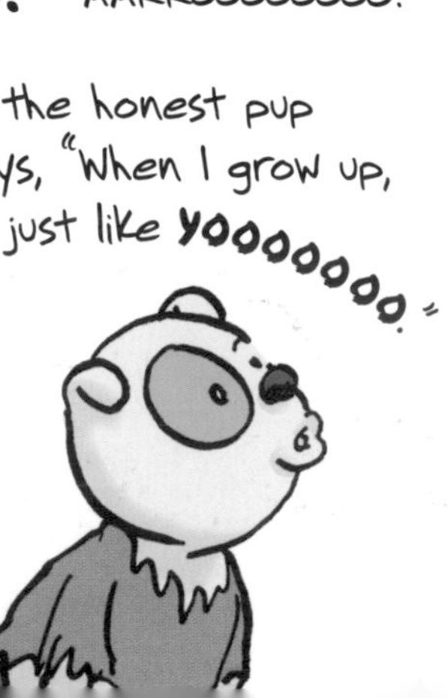

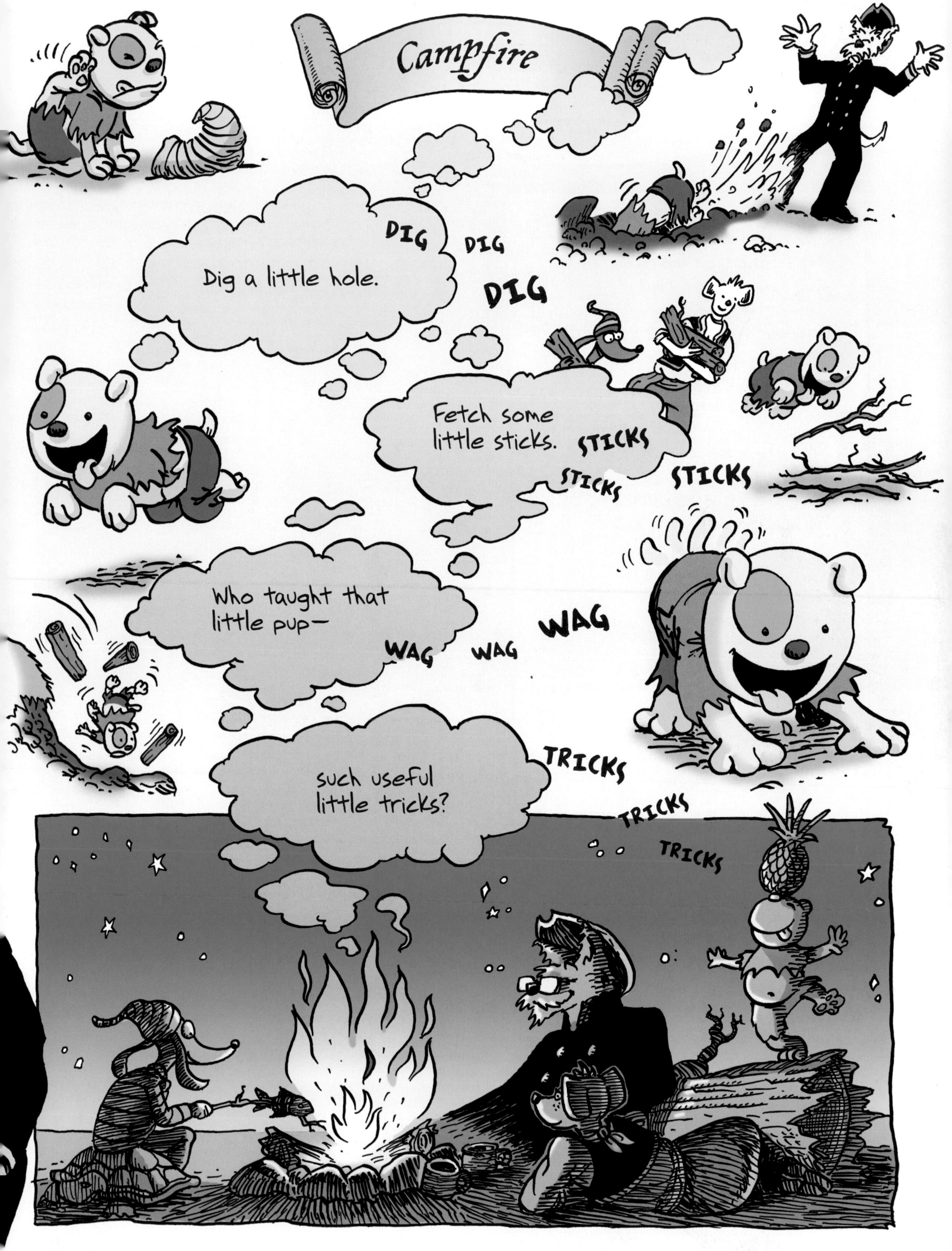
Campfire
Dig a little hole.
DIG
DIG
DIG
Fetch some little sticks.
STICKS
STICKS
STICKS
Who taught that little pup—
WAG
WAG
WAG
such useful little tricks?
TRICKS
TRICKS
TRICKS

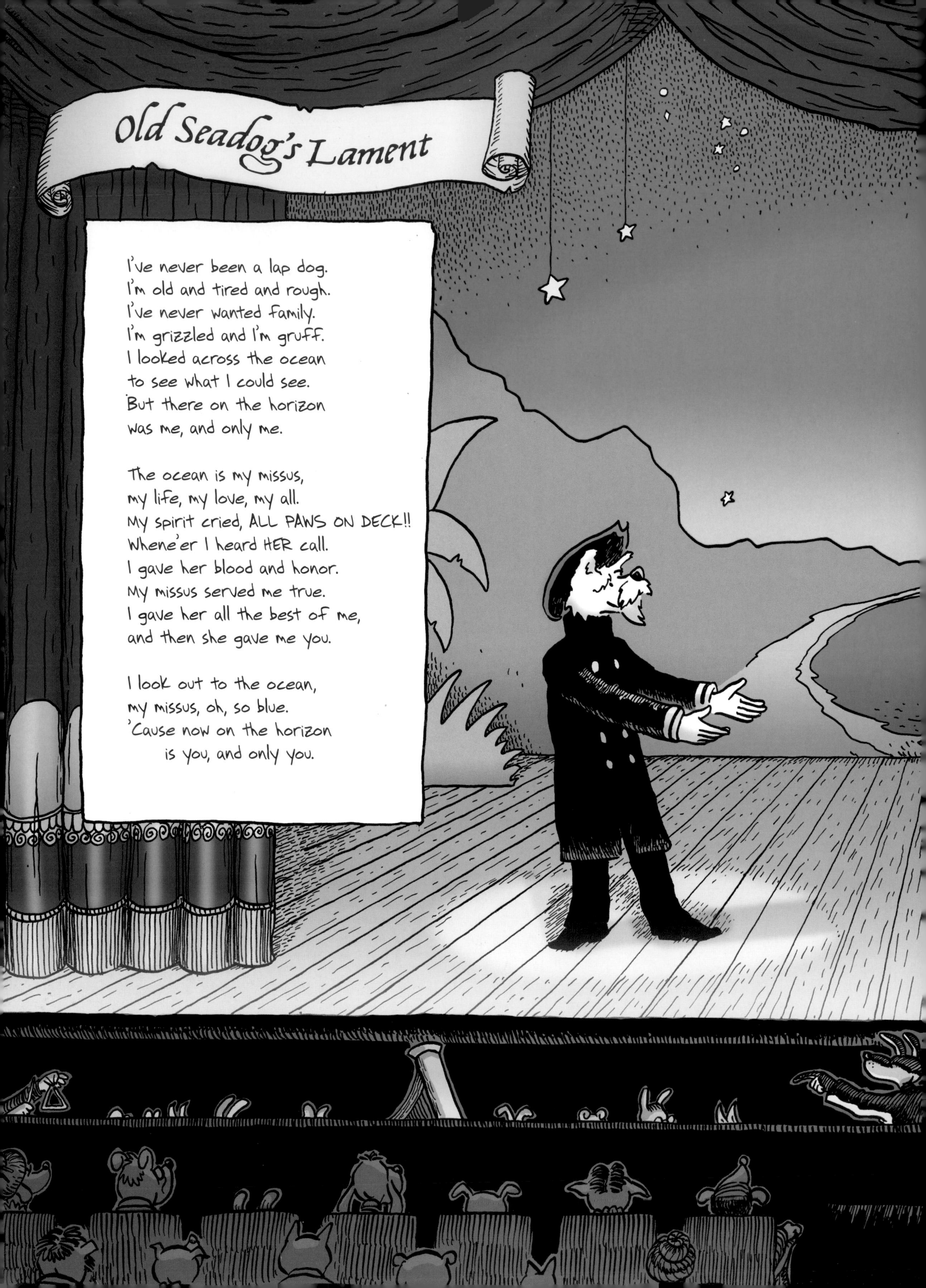
Old Seadog's Lament
I've never been a lap dog.
I'm old and tired and rough.
I've never wanted family.
I'm grizzled and I'm gruff.
I looked across the ocean
to see what I could see.
But there on the horizon
was me, and only me.

The ocean is my missus,
my life, my love, my all.
My spirit cried, ALL PAWS ON DECK!!
Whene'er I heard HER call.
I gave her blood and honor.
My missus served me true.
I gave her all the best of me,
and then she gave me you.

I look out to the ocean,
my missus, oh, so blue.
'Cause now on the horizon
is you, and only you.

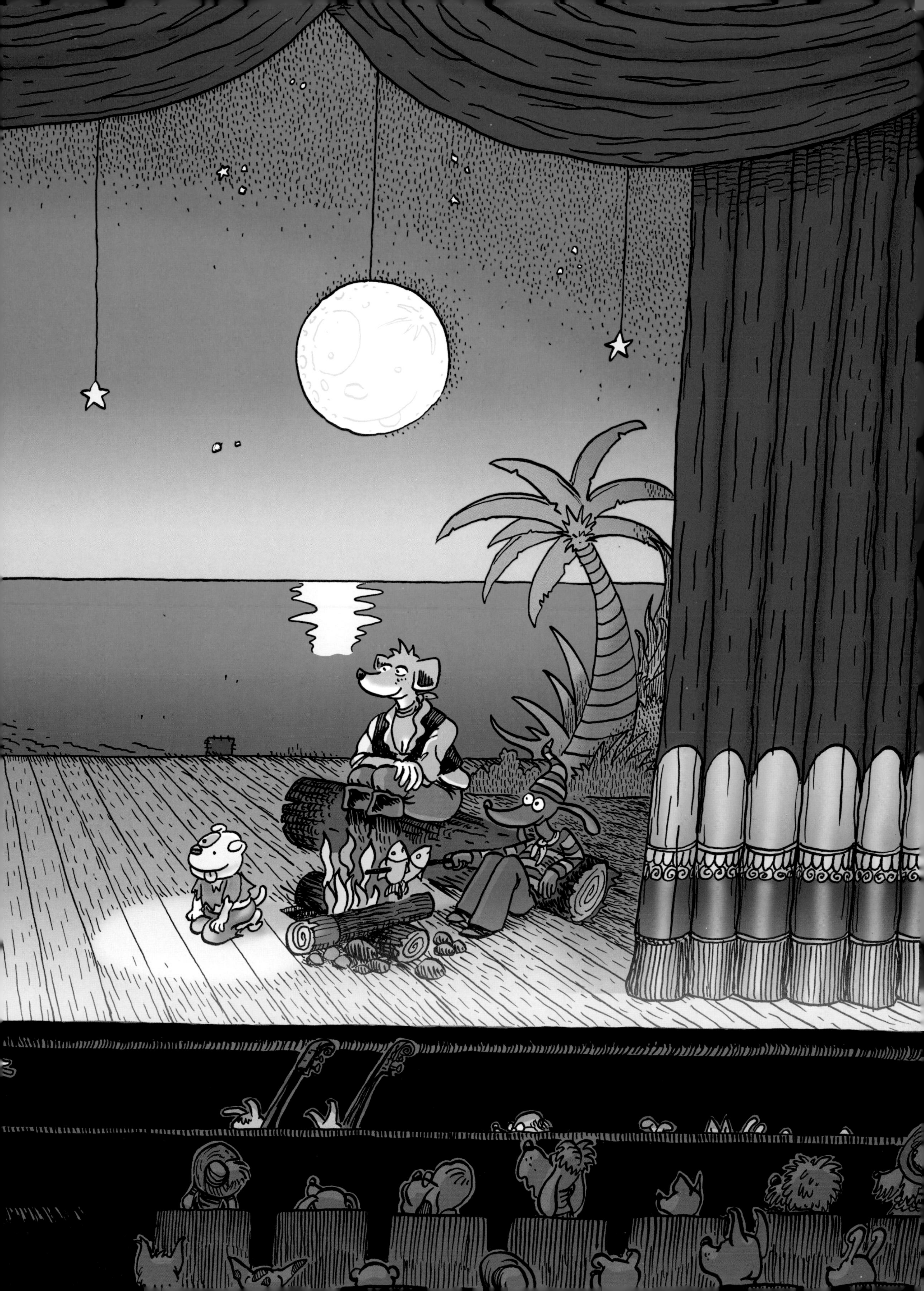

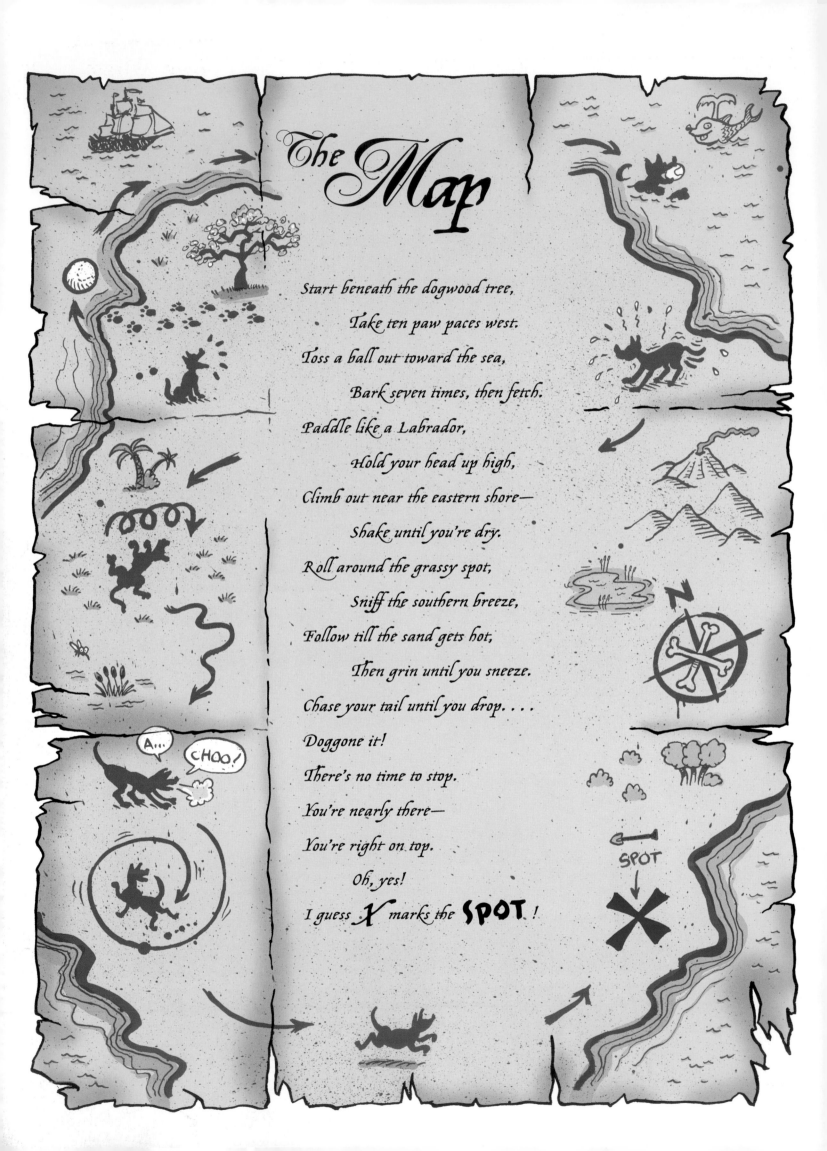

The Map

Start beneath the dogwood tree,
Take ten paw paces west.
Toss a ball out toward the sea,
Bark seven times, then fetch.
Paddle like a Labrador,
Hold your head up high,
Climb out near the eastern shore—
Shake until you're dry.
Roll around the grassy spot,
Sniff the southern breeze,
Follow till the sand gets hot,
Then grin until you sneeze.
Chase your tail until you drop. . . .
Doggone it!
There's no time to stop.
You're nearly there—
You're right on top.
Oh, yes!
I guess X marks the **SPOT**!

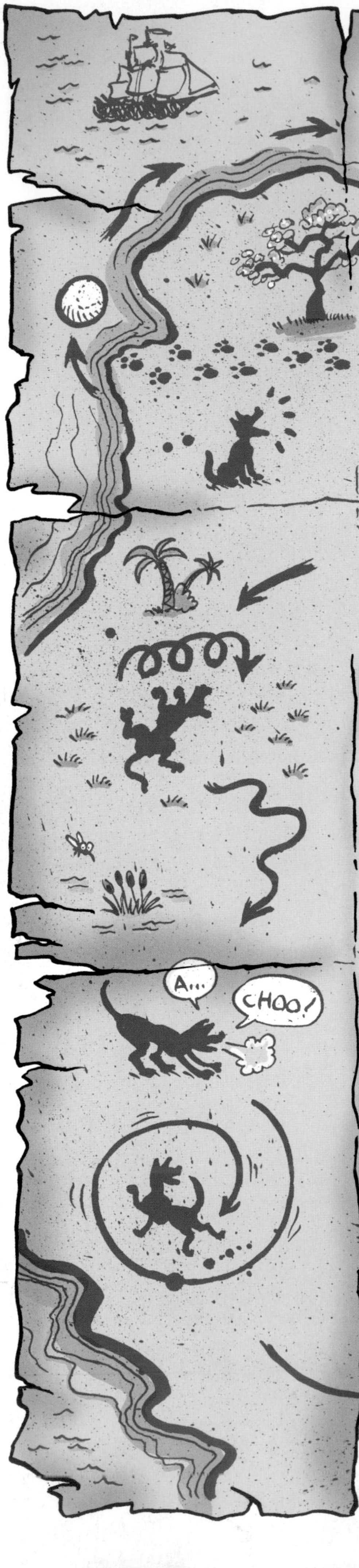
A...
CHOO!

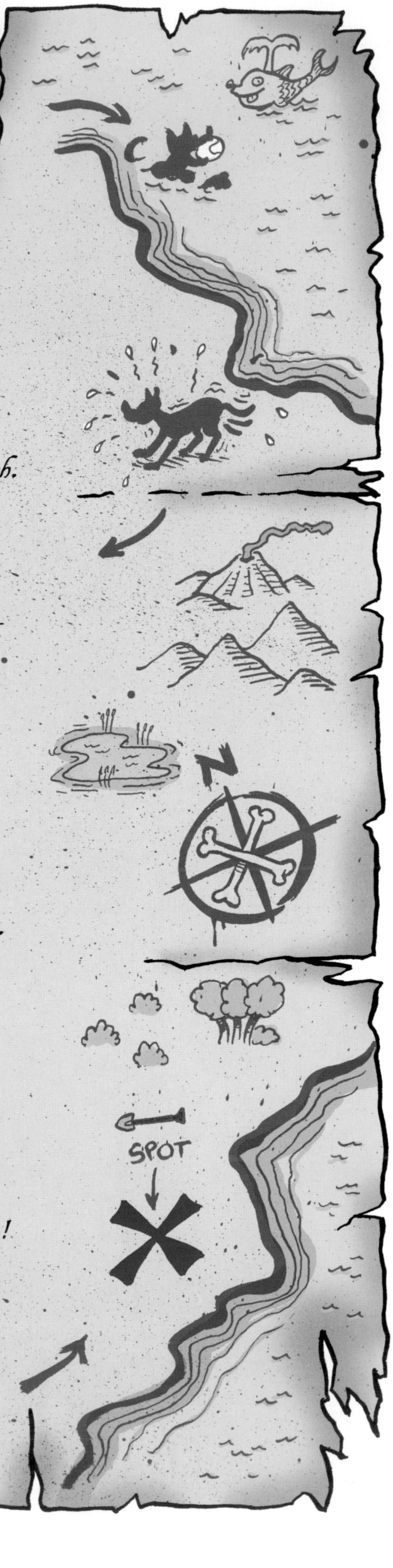
SPOT

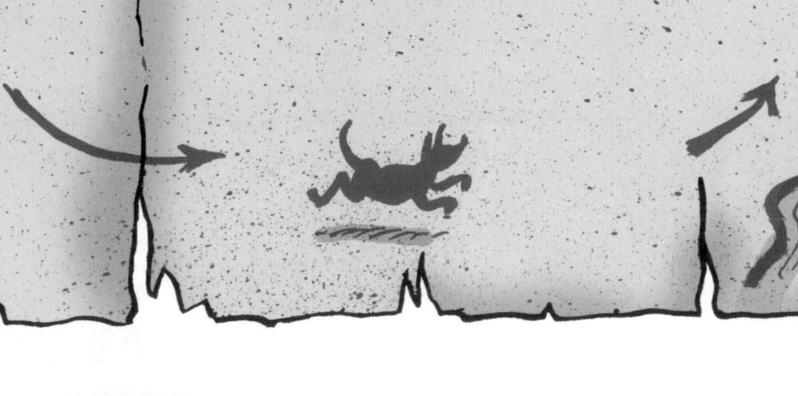

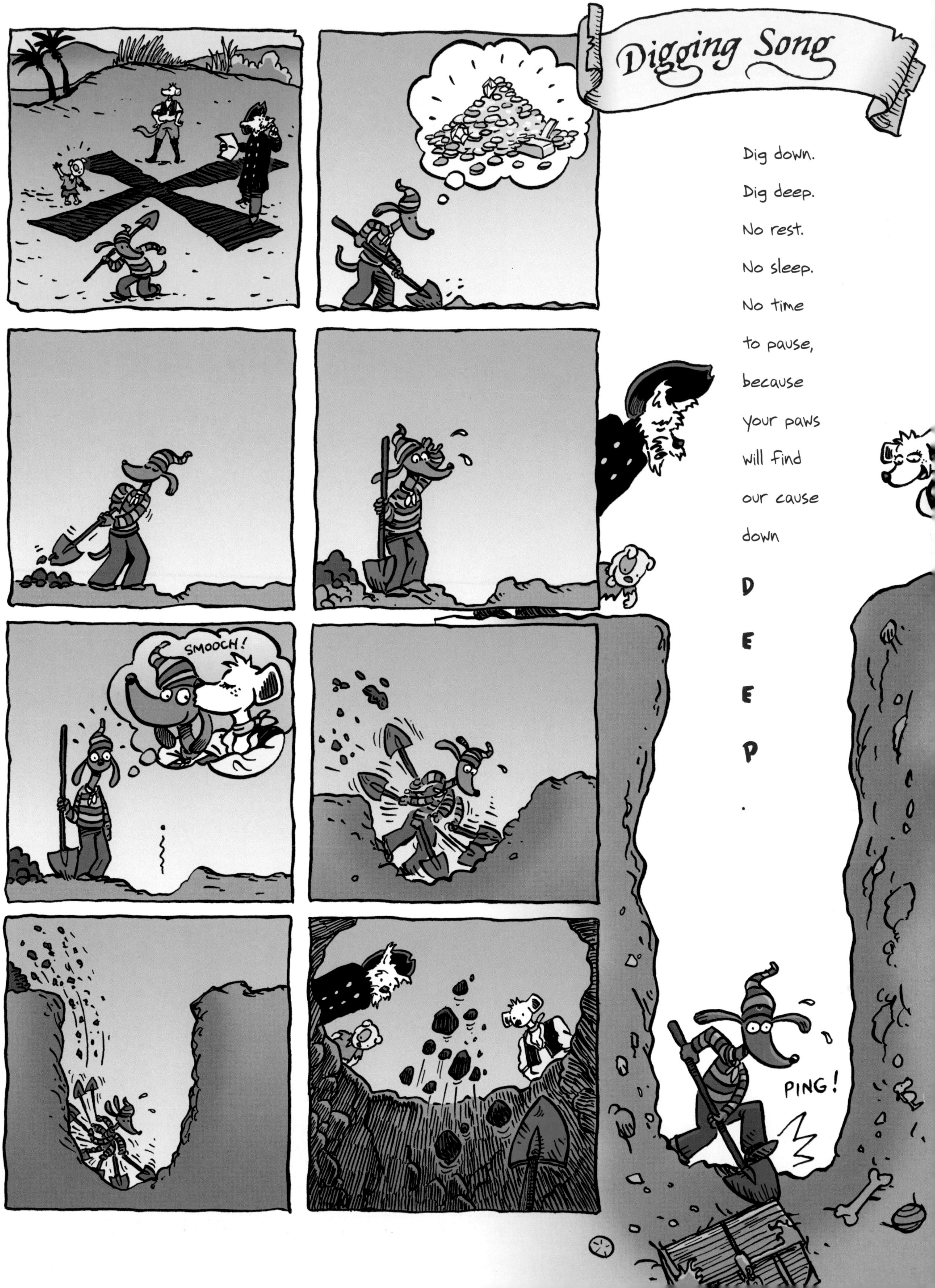
Digging Song
Dig down.
Dig deep.
No rest.
No sleep.
No time
to pause,
because
your paws
will find
our cause
down
D
E
E
P
.
SMOOCH!
PING!

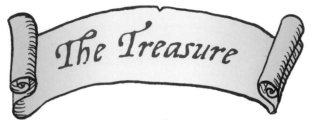

The Treasure

Oh! Look, look, look!
There's something there.
A box? A crate?
A chest so rare?

Haul it up. Pull it up.
H-e-a-v-e, ho!
Careful—Three more feet to go. . . .

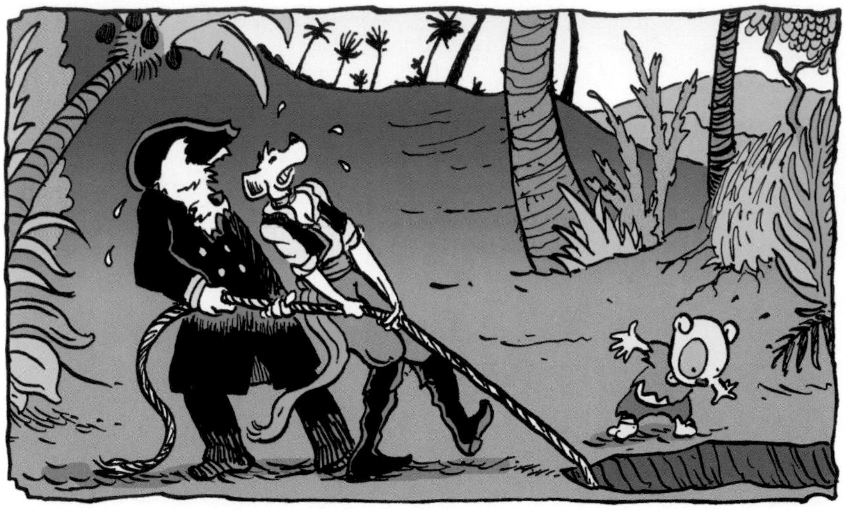

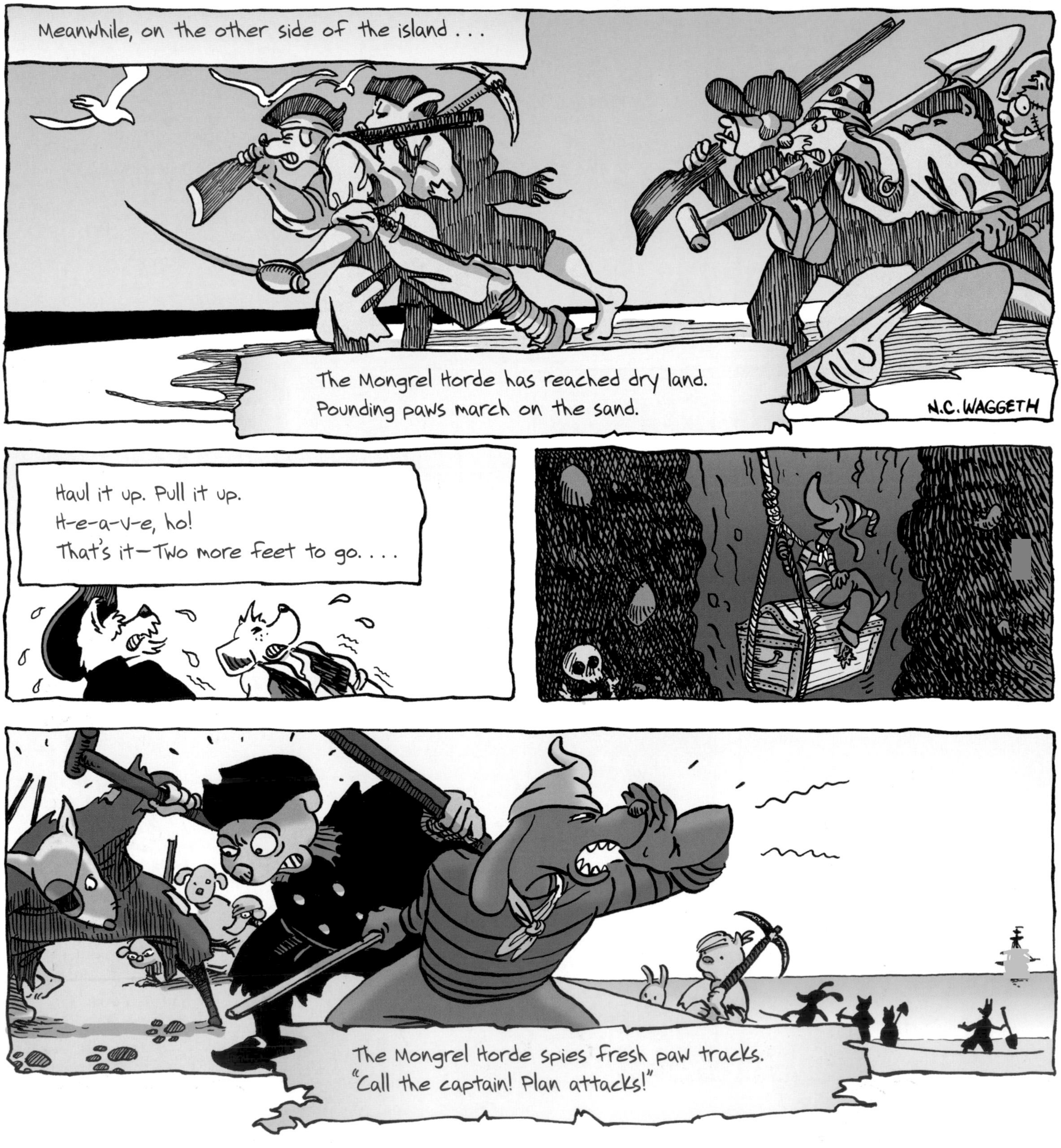

Meanwhile, on the other side of the island . . .
The Mongrel Horde has reached dry land.
Pounding paws march on the sand.
N.C. WAGGETH
Haul it up. Pull it up.
H-e-a-v-e, ho!
That's it—Two more feet to go. . . .
The Mongrel Horde spies fresh paw tracks.
"Call the captain! Plan attacks!"

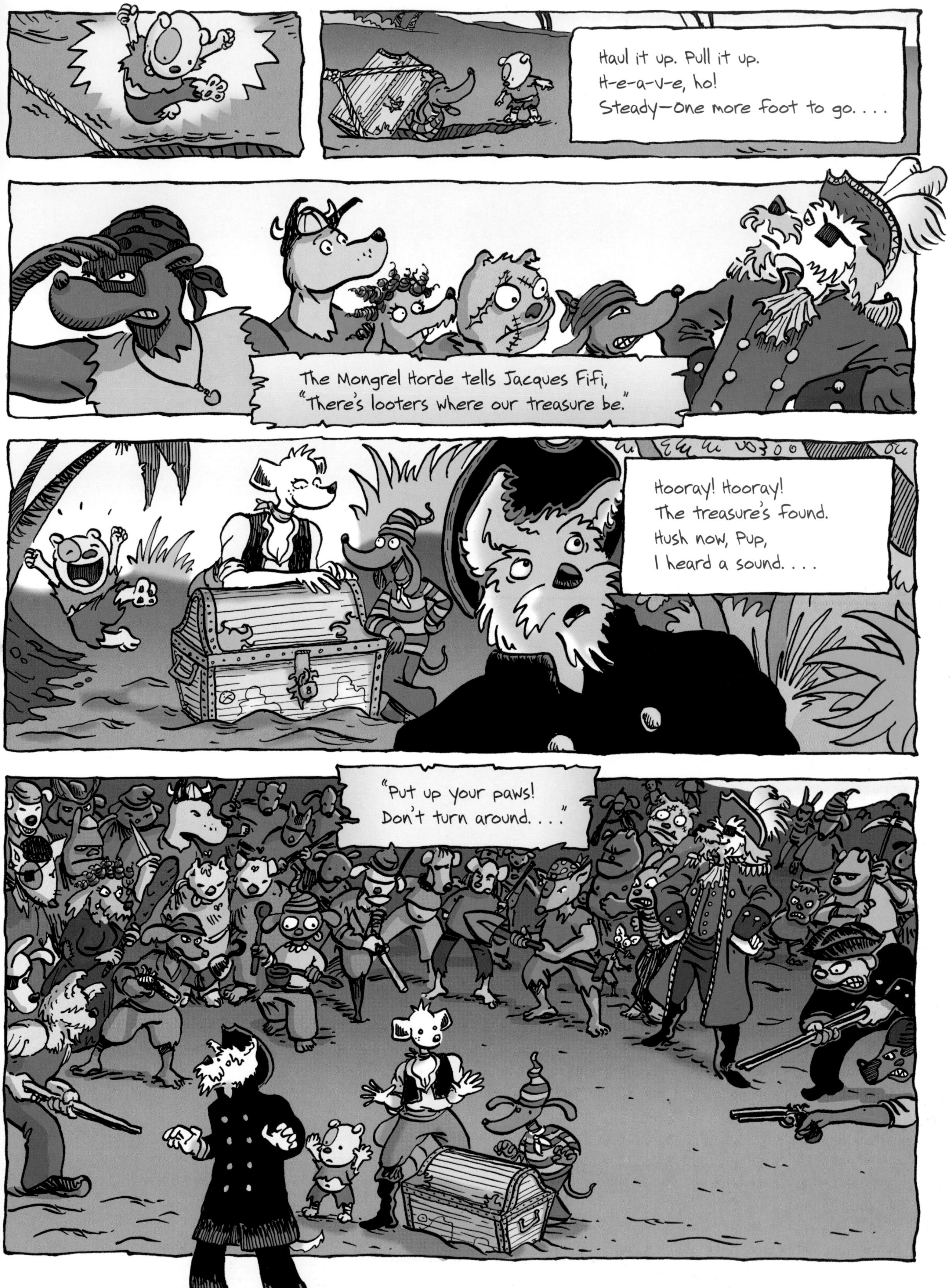
Haul it up. Pull it up.
H-e-a-v-e, ho!
Steady—one more foot to go. . . .
The Mongrel Horde tells Jacques Fifi,
"There's looters where our treasure be."
Hooray! Hooray!
The treasure's found.
Hush now, Pup,
I heard a sound. . . .
"Put up your paws!
Don't turn around. . . ."

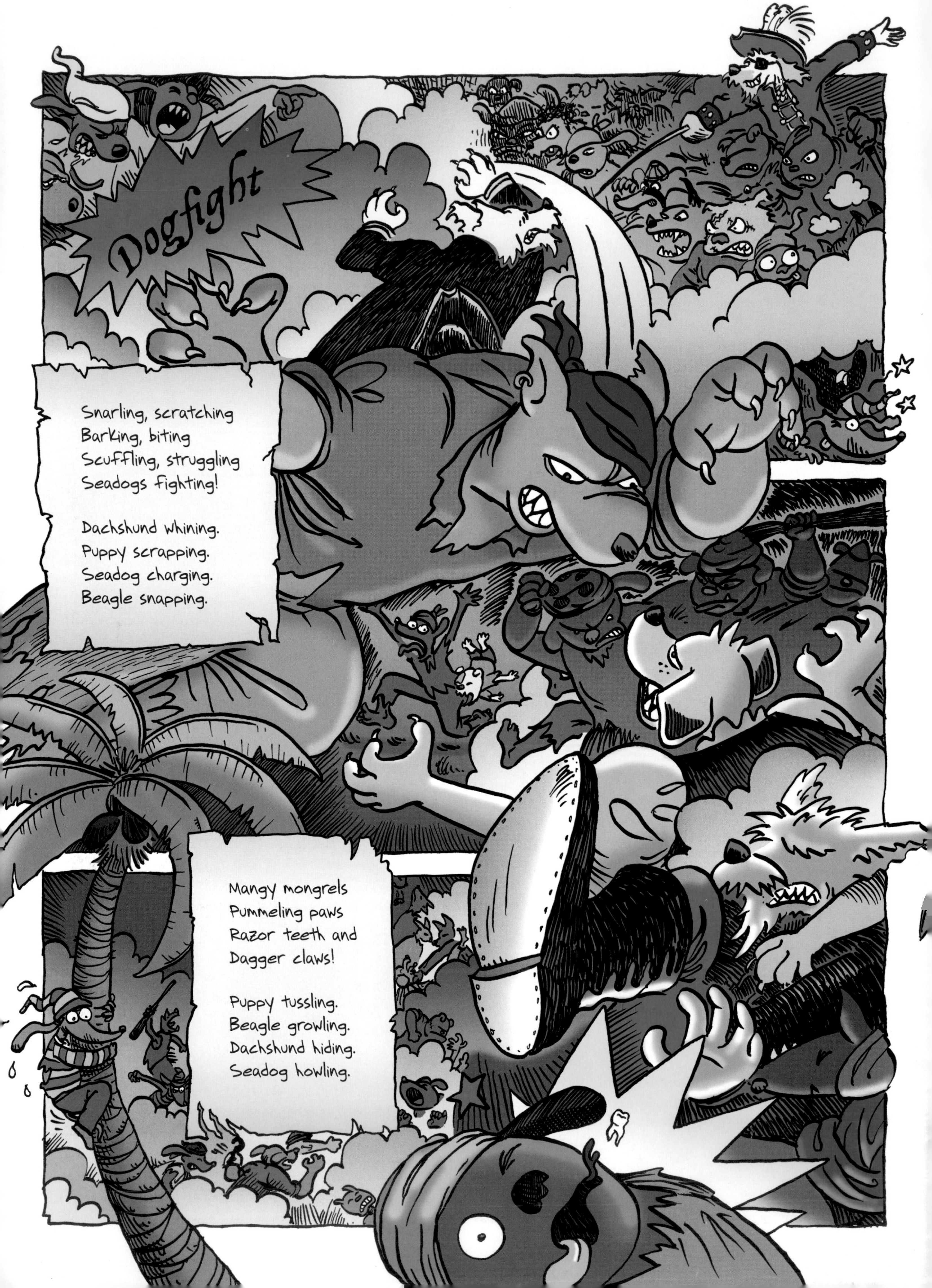
Dogfight
Snarling, scratching
Barking, biting
Scuffling, struggling
Seadogs fighting!
Dachshund whining.
Puppy scrapping.
Seadog charging.
Beagle snapping.
Mangy mongrels
Pummeling paws
Razor teeth and
Dagger claws!
Puppy tussling.
Beagle growling.
Dachshund hiding.
Seadog howling.

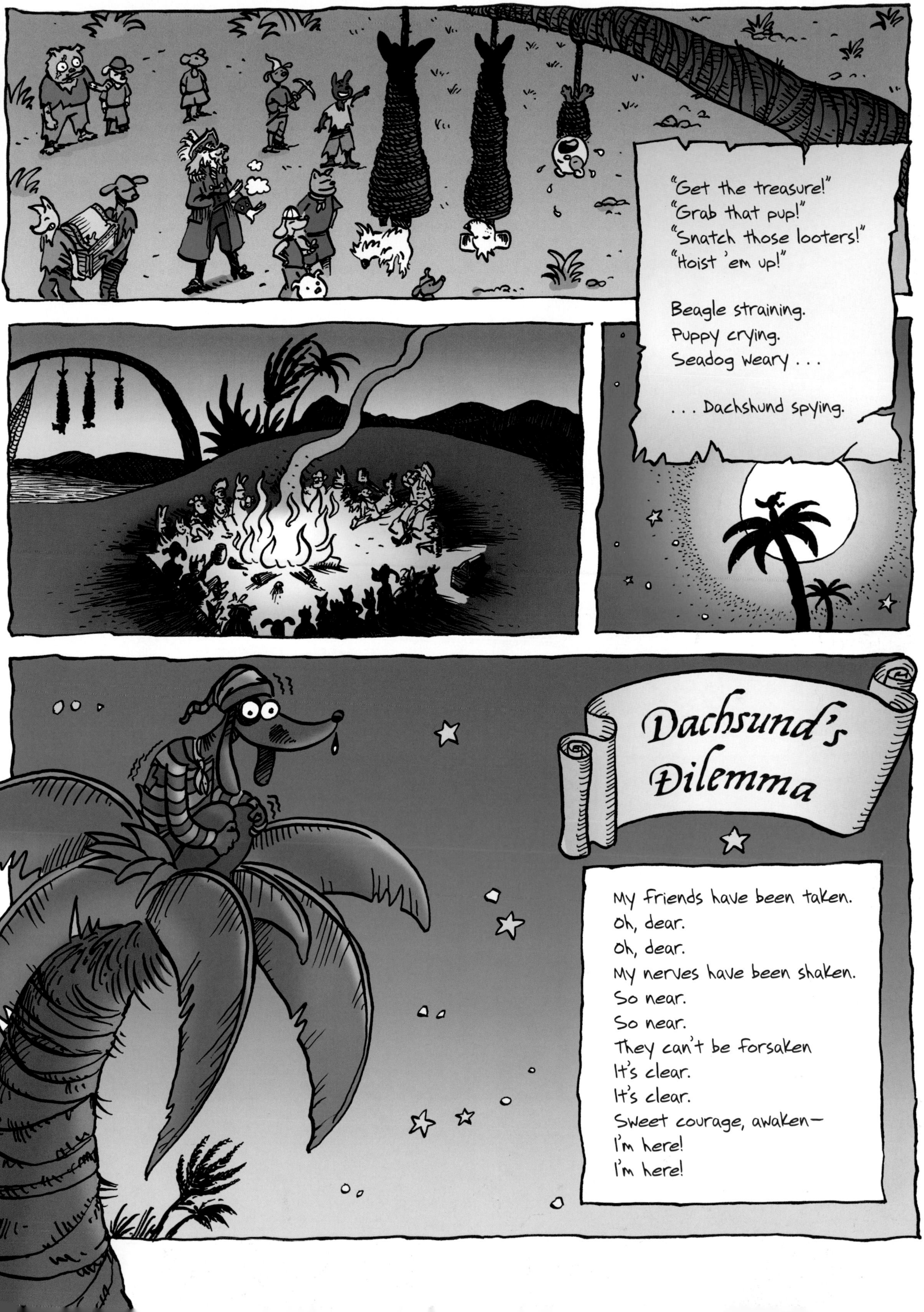
"Get the treasure!"
"Grab that pup!"
"Snatch those looters!"
"Hoist 'em up!"
Beagle straining.
Puppy crying.
Seadog weary . . .
. . . Dachshund spying.
Dachsund's Dilemma
My friends have been taken.
Oh, dear.
Oh, dear.
My nerves have been shaken.
So near.
So near.
They can't be forsaken
It's clear.
It's clear.
Sweet courage, awaken—
I'm here!
I'm here!

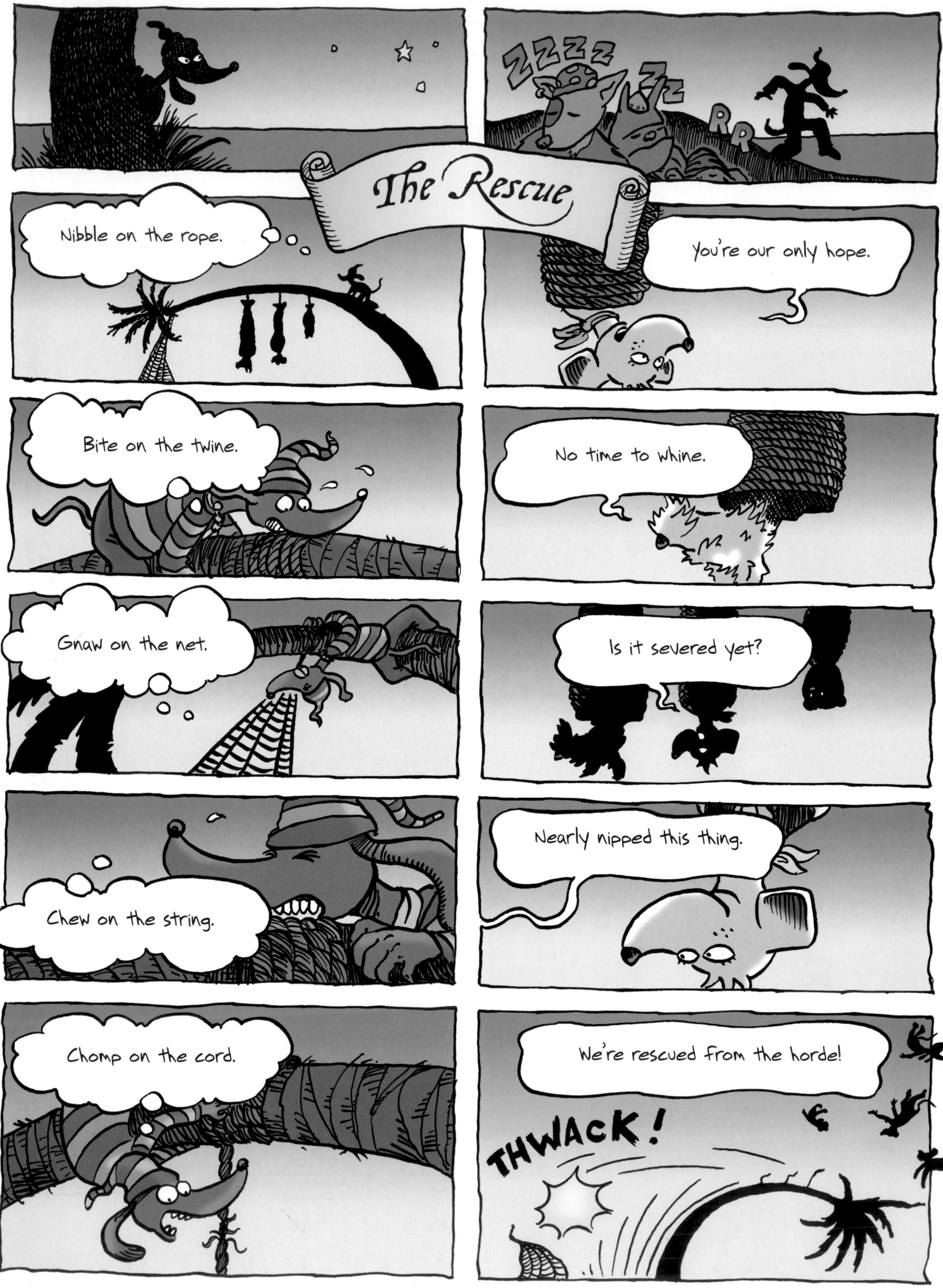
The Rescue
ZZZZ
ZZ
RR
Nibble on the rope.
You're our only hope.
Bite on the twine.
No time to whine.
Gnaw on the net.
Is it severed yet?
Chew on the string.
Nearly nipped this thing.
Chomp on the cord.
We're rescued from the horde!
THWACK!

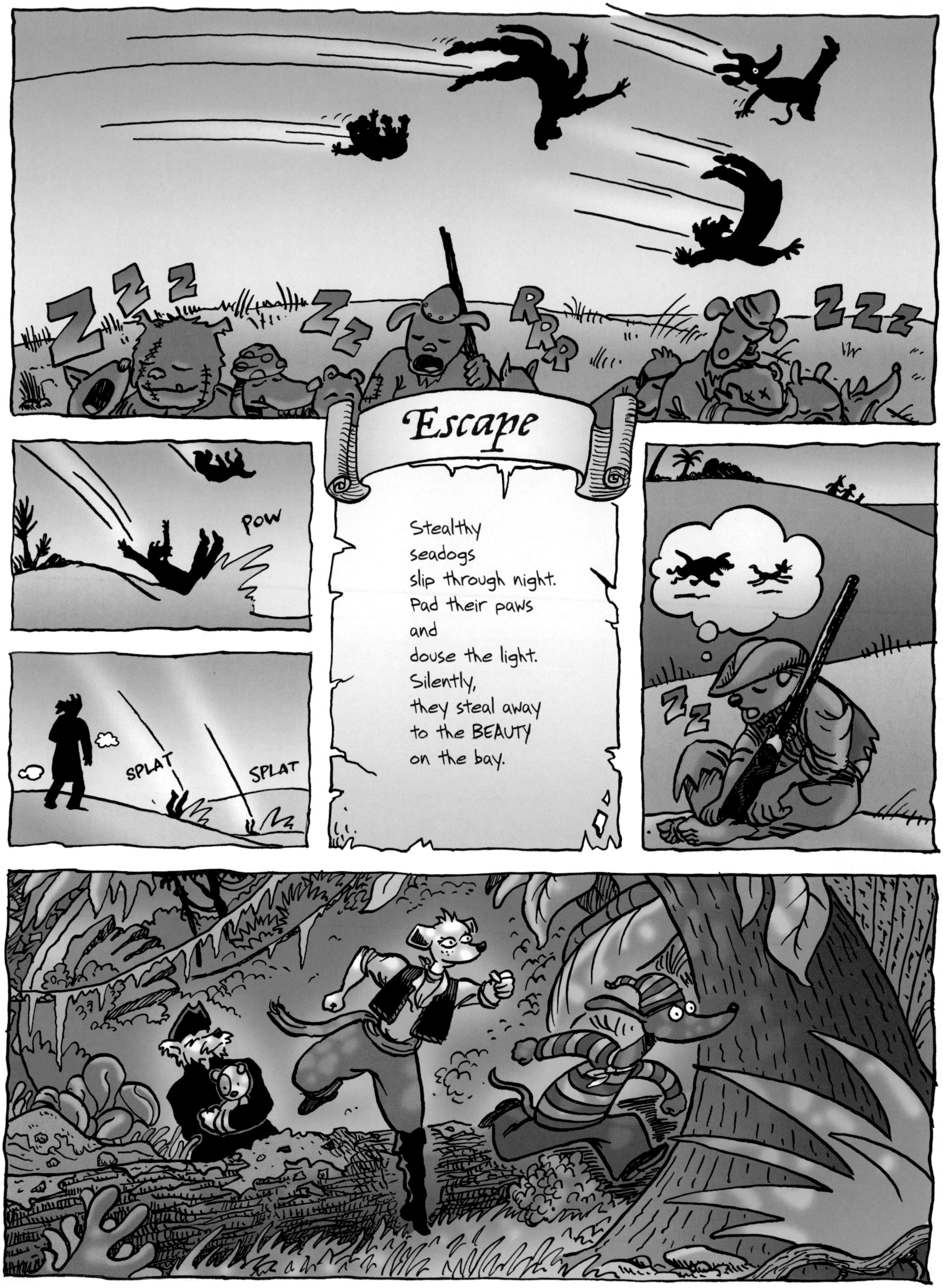
Z Z Z
Z Z
RRR
Z Z Z
Escape
POW
SPLAT
SPLAT
Stealthy
seadogs
slip through night.
Pad their paws
and
douse the light.
Silently,
they steal away
to the BEAUTY
on the bay.
Z Z

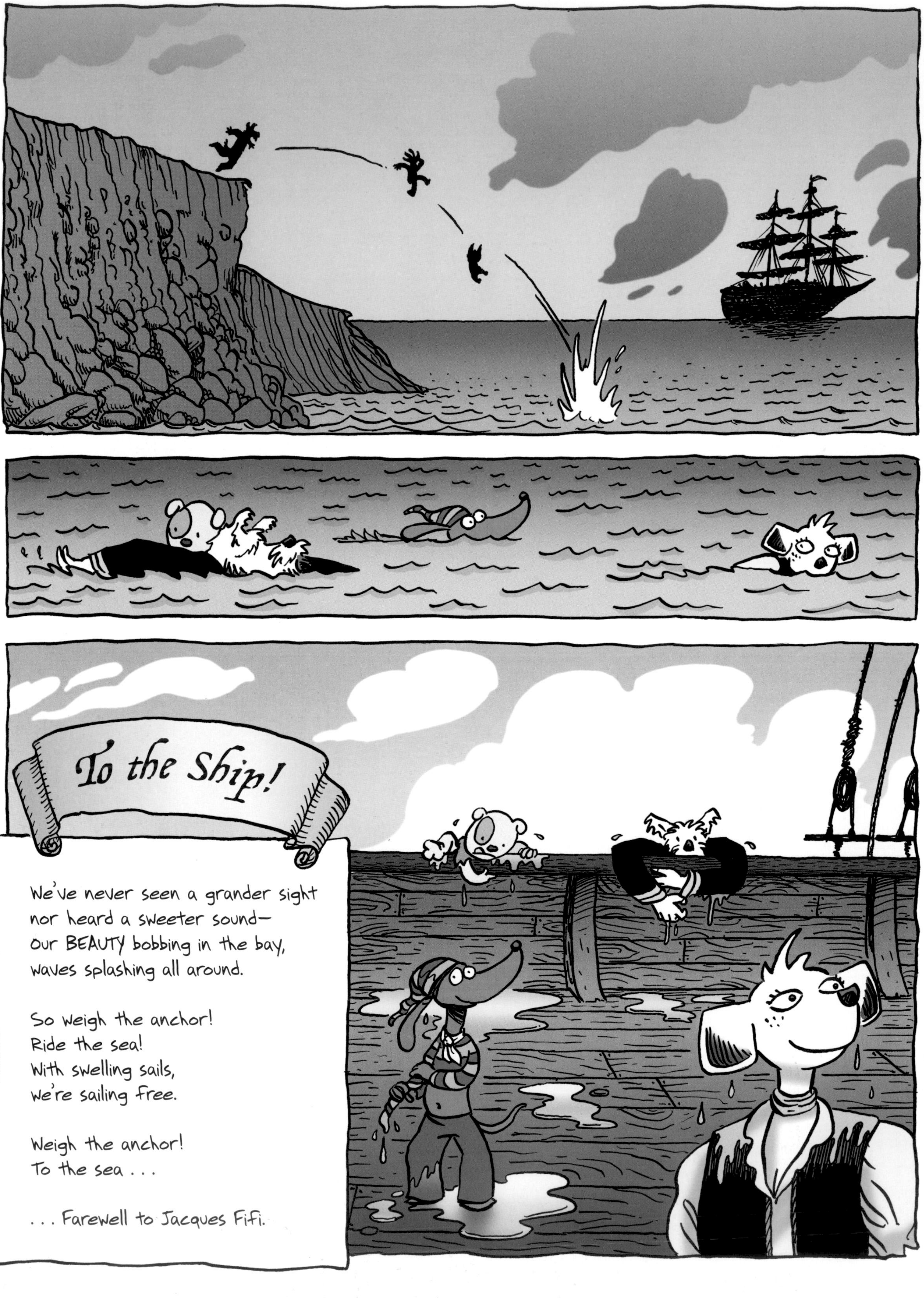
To the Ship!
We've never seen a grander sight
nor heard a sweeter sound—
our BEAUTY bobbing in the bay,
waves splashing all around.

So weigh the anchor!
Ride the sea!
With swelling sails,
we're sailing free.

Weigh the anchor!
To the sea . . .

. . . Farewell to Jacques Fifi.

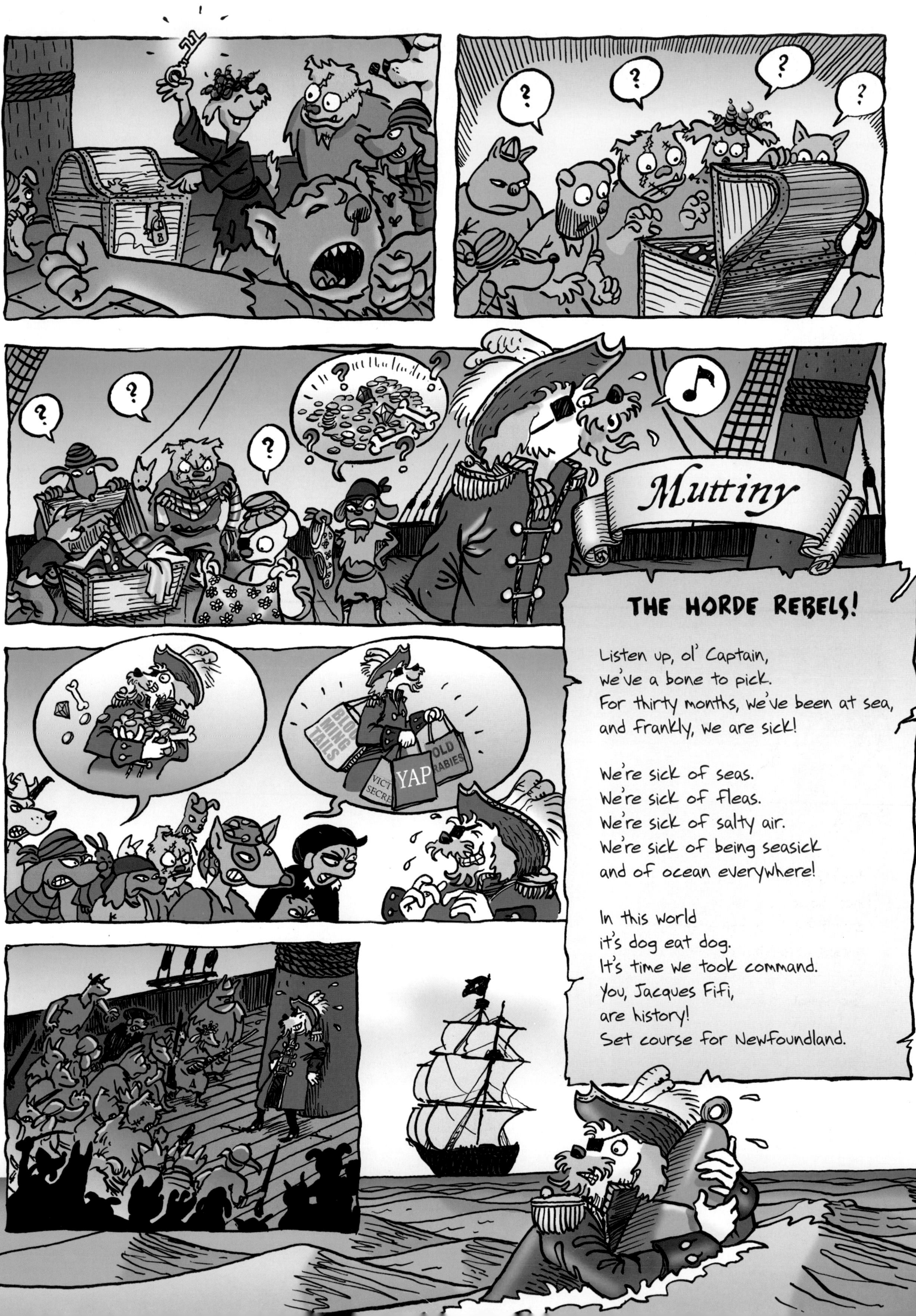
Muttiny
THE HORDE REBELS!
Listen up, ol' Captain,
we've a bone to pick.
For thirty months, we've been at sea,
and frankly, we are sick!

We're sick of seas.
We're sick of fleas.
We're sick of salty air.
We're sick of being seasick
and of ocean everywhere!

In this world
it's dog eat dog.
It's time we took command.
You, Jacques Fifi,
are history!
Set course for Newfoundland.
YAP
OLD RABIES

Homeward Bound

If sails and ropes
were dreams and hopes,
we'd be a merry crew.

If salt and brine
meant suppertime,
we'd have a meal to chew.

If gulls and fish
could grant each wish,
we'd never want for more.

And if the foam
should call us home,
we'll meet you on the shore, the shore . . .

. . . that heavenly distant shore.

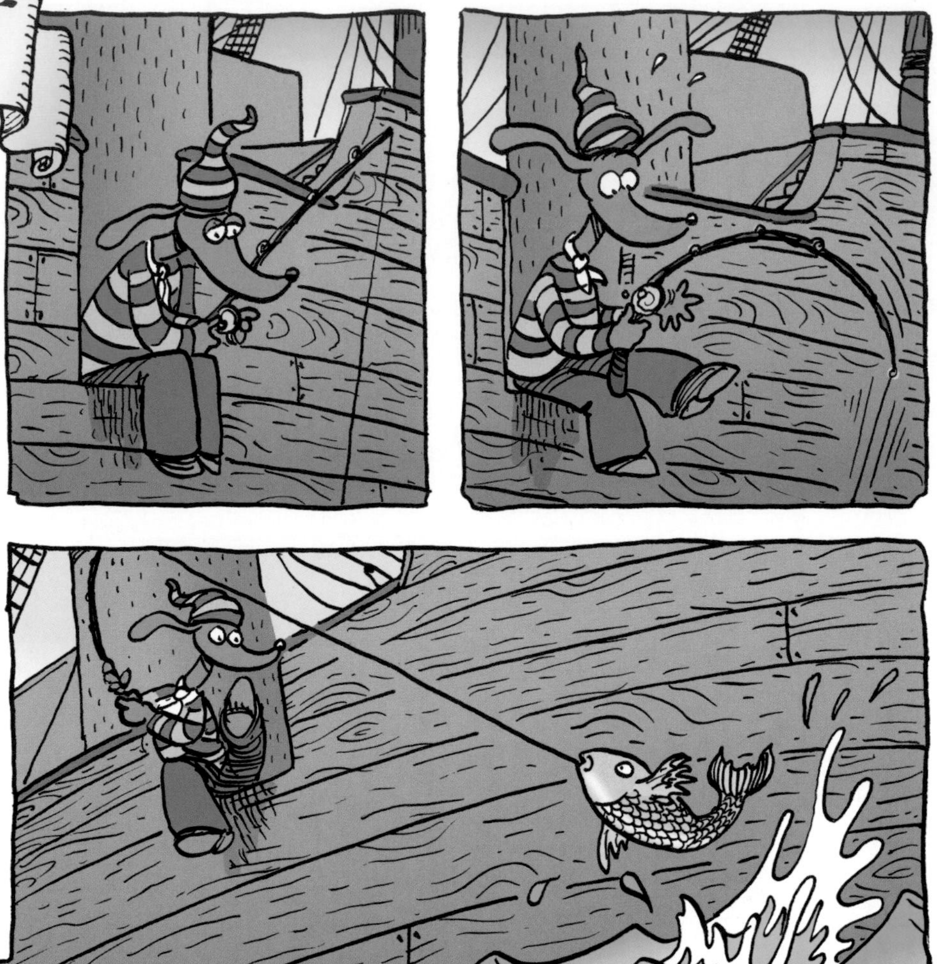

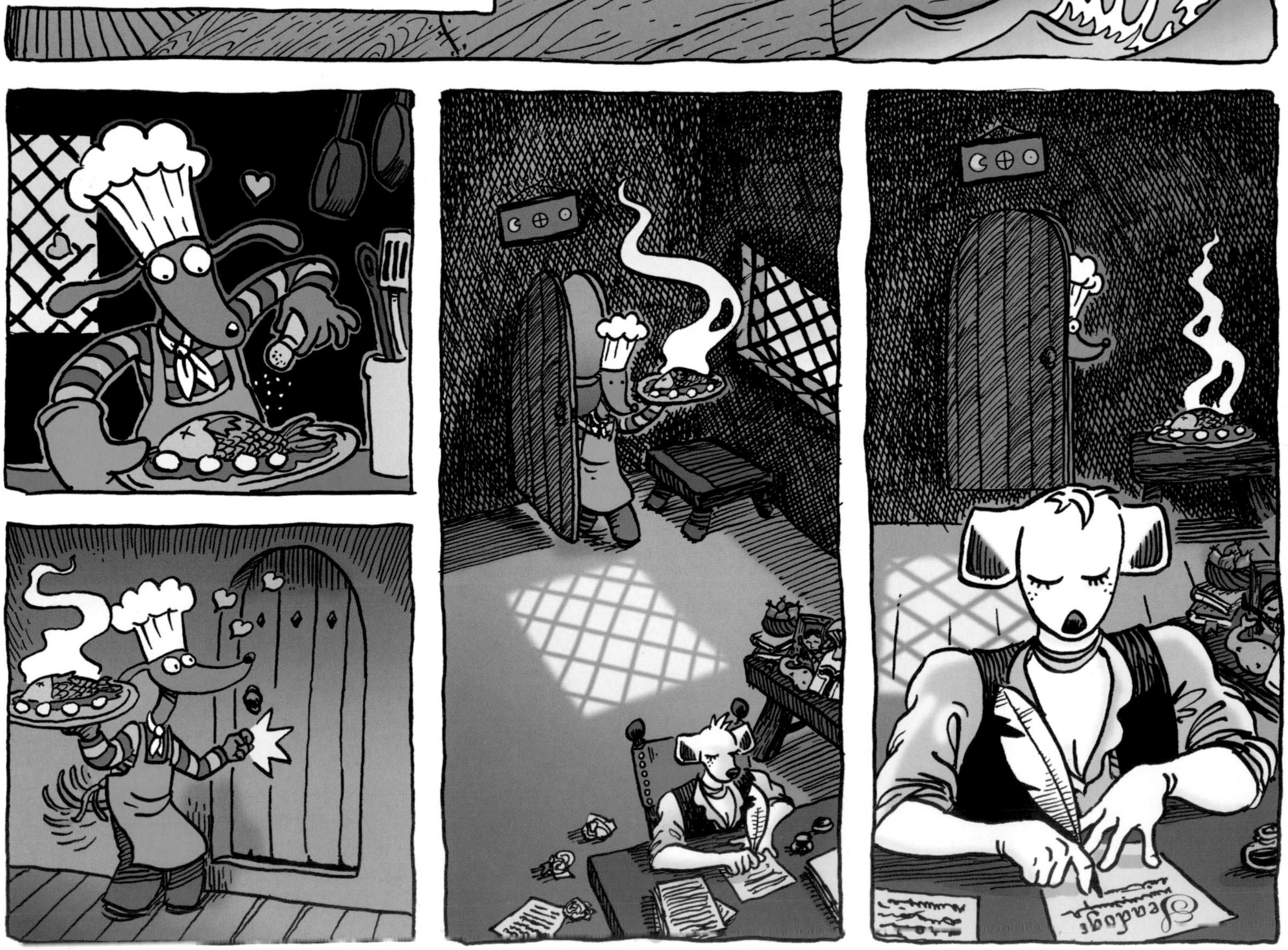

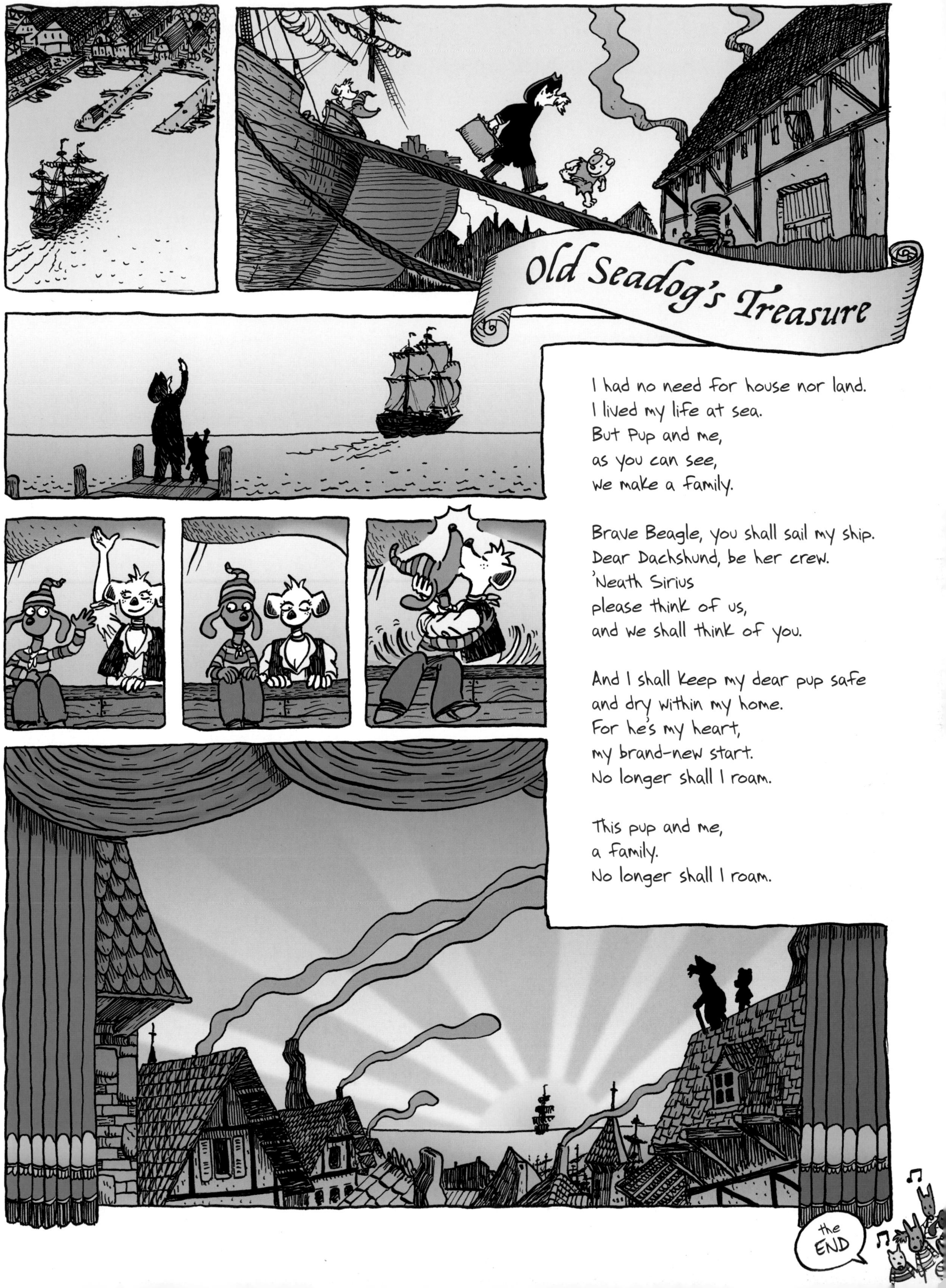
Old Seadog's Treasure
I had no need for house nor land.
I lived my life at sea.
But Pup and me,
as you can see,
we make a family.

Brave Beagle, you shall sail my ship.
Dear Dachshund, be her crew.
'Neath Sirius
please think of us,
and we shall think of you.

And I shall keep my dear pup safe
and dry within my home.
For he's my heart,
my brand-new start.
No longer shall I roam.

This pup and me,
a family.
No longer shall I roam.
the END

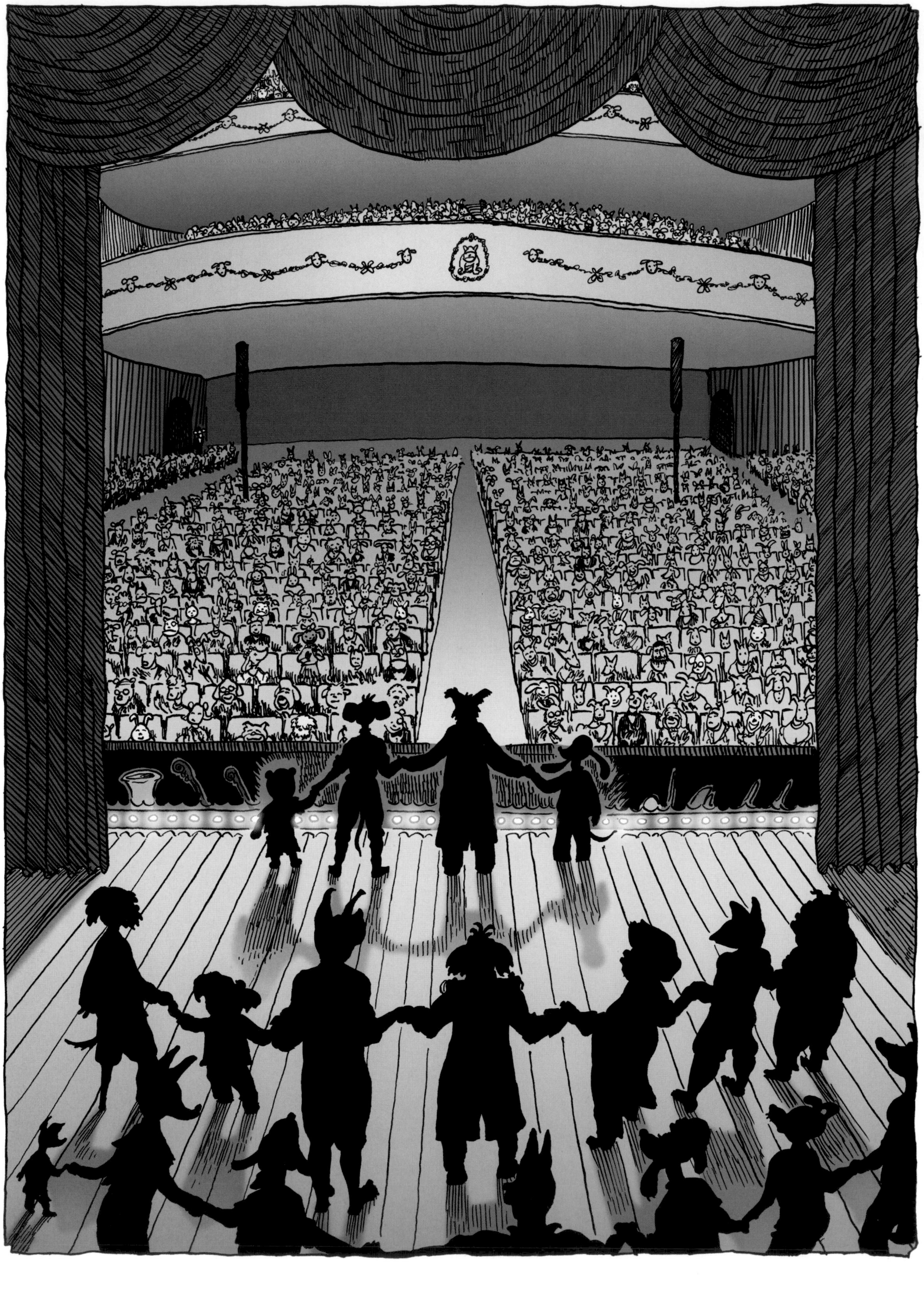

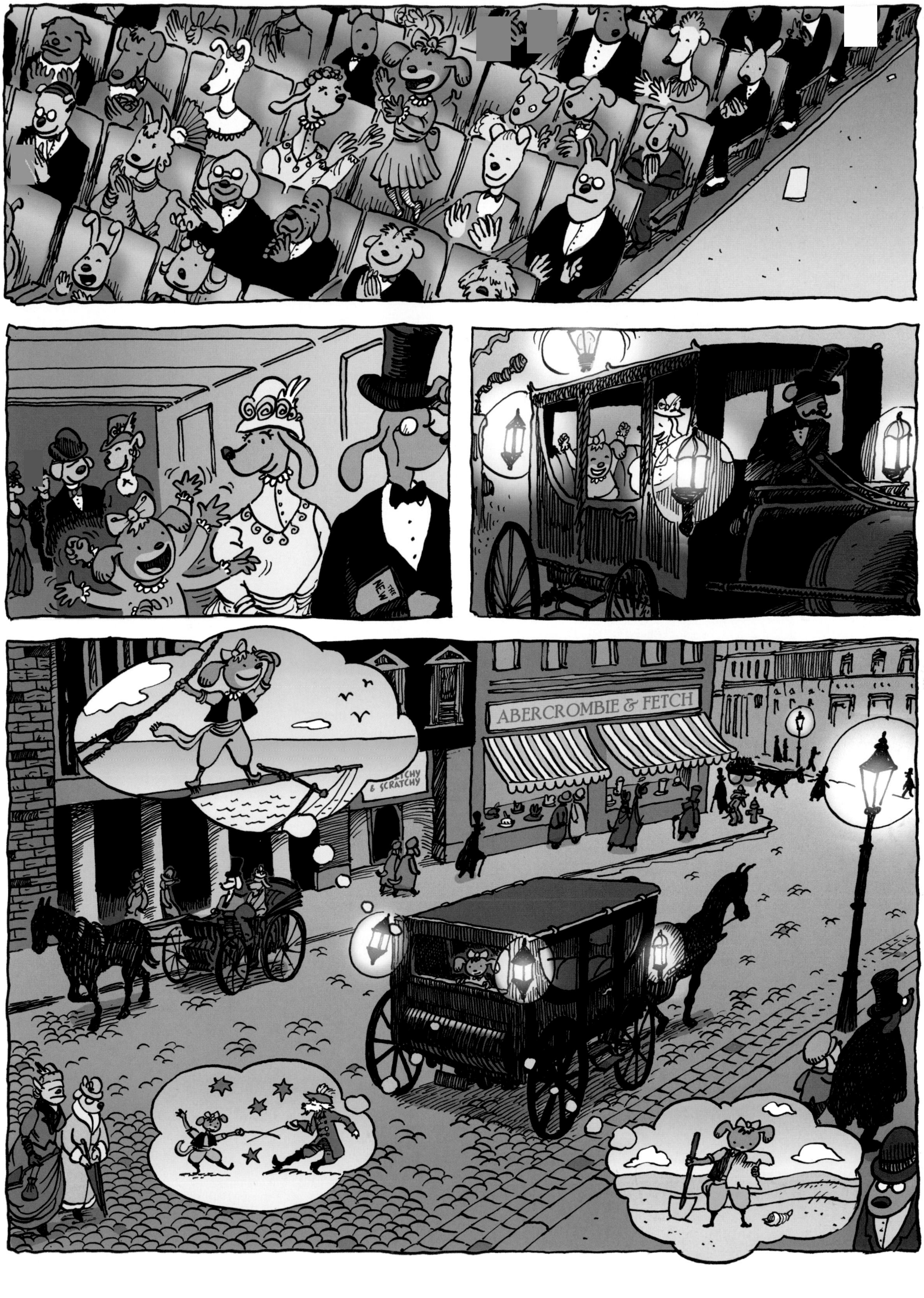
THE NEW
ABERCROMBIE & FETCH
& SCRATCHY

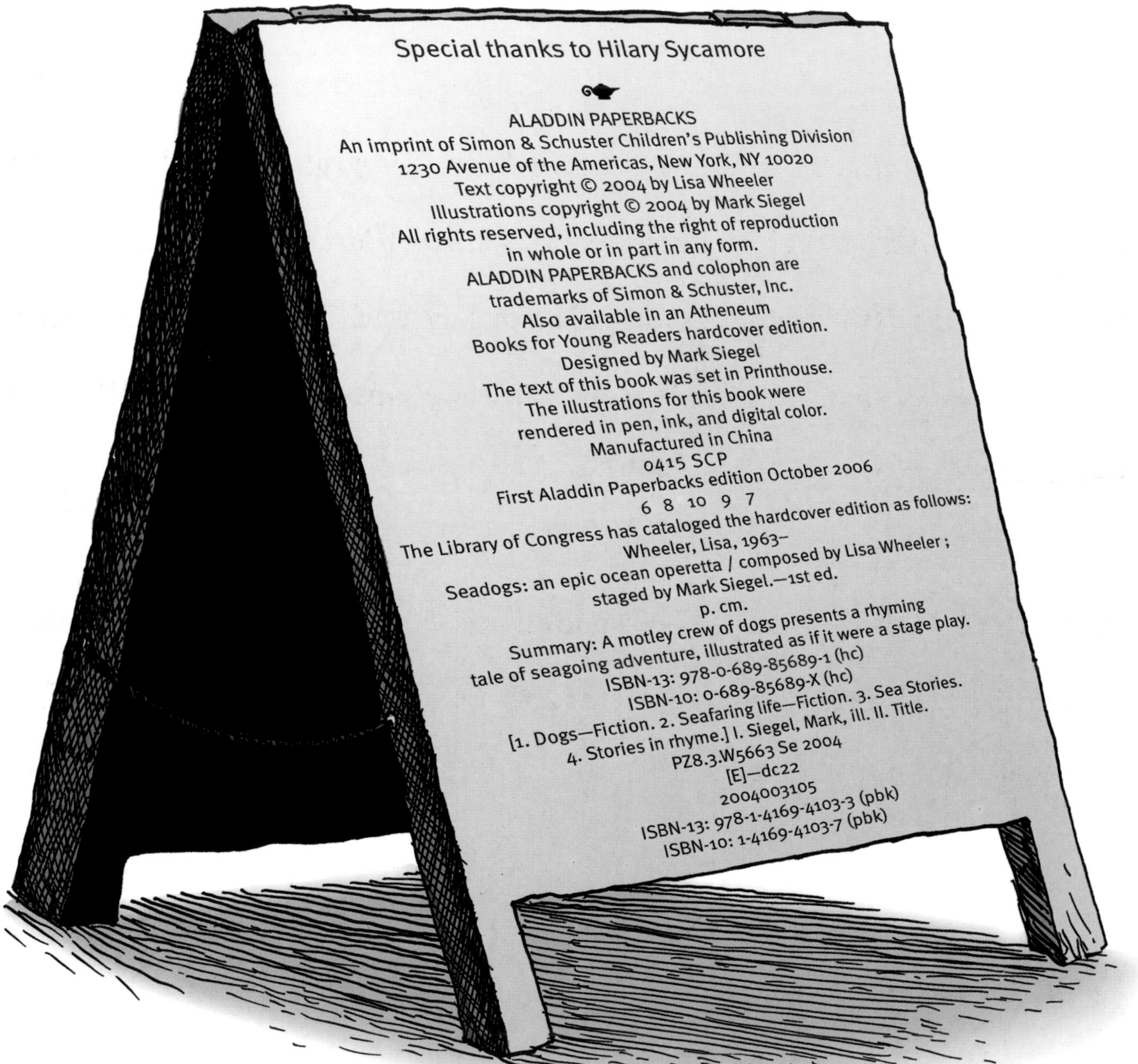
Special thanks to Hilary Sycamore
ALADDIN PAPERBACKS
An imprint of Simon & Schuster Children's Publishing Division
1230 Avenue of the Americas, New York, NY 10020
Text copyright © 2004 by Lisa Wheeler
Illustrations copyright © 2004 by Mark Siegel
All rights reserved, including the right of reproduction
in whole or in part in any form.
ALADDIN PAPERBACKS and colophon are
trademarks of Simon & Schuster, Inc.
Also available in an Atheneum
Books for Young Readers hardcover edition.
Designed by Mark Siegel
The text of this book was set in Printhouse.
The illustrations for this book were
rendered in pen, ink, and digital color.
Manufactured in China
0415 SCP
First Aladdin Paperbacks edition October 2006
6 8 10 9 7
The Library of Congress has cataloged the hardcover edition as follows:
Wheeler, Lisa, 1963–
Seadogs: an epic ocean operetta / composed by Lisa Wheeler ;
staged by Mark Siegel.—1st ed.
p. cm.
Summary: A motley crew of dogs presents a rhyming
tale of seagoing adventure, illustrated as if it were a stage play.
ISBN-13: 978-0-689-85689-1 (hc)
ISBN-10: 0-689-85689-X (hc)
[1. Dogs—Fiction. 2. Seafaring life—Fiction. 3. Sea Stories.
4. Stories in rhyme.] I. Siegel, Mark, ill. II. Title.
PZ8.3.W5663 Se 2004
[E]—dc22
2004003105
ISBN-13: 978-1-4169-4103-3 (pbk)
ISBN-10: 1-4169-4103-7 (pbk)